♥

CHECK MATES

♥

Jessamy tapped her fingers against her chin, considering her next move, and then extricated herself from check.

"I believe we can consider this a draw," Rand said, and she agreed. "You're quite good," he added softly. "I had not thought you could hold out against me. You are quite a woman, Jessamy Montgomery."

"I shall choose to take that as a compliment."

"It is. I've never met a woman quite like you."

"I should think not, my lord." She took a sip of claret.

"Don't call me that!" he flared. "I'm an American."

"So I noticed." Jessamy gazed at Rand over the rim of her goblet....But how could she speak when he was so close? Her heart began to thud, and she found it difficult to breathe with him so near.

Then Rand was reaching out to stroke her face with the backs of his fingers.

"You're quite lovely," he murmured, "but I suppose you know that."

He was going to kiss her, Jessamy knew then, and didn't know whether to retreat or stay; but then the decision was taken from her as Rand leaned forward, his mouth touching her lips...

Love's Gambit

Love's Gambit

EMMA HARRINGTON

WARNER BOOKS

A Warner Communications Company

PB
H
#1

WARNER BOOKS EDITION

This Warner Books Edition is published by arrangement with
Wildstar Books, a division of the Adele Leone Agency, Inc.

Warner Books, Inc.
666 Fifth Avenue
New York, N.Y. 10103

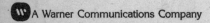 A Warner Communications Company

Printed in the United States of America

First Printing: January, 1988

10 9 8 7 6 5 4 3 2 1

DEDICATED TO

The *Kids* who put up with your moms'
constant pecking on the keys—

Micki, Eric, Jack, Ben, and Joey

✳ Chapter 1 ✳

Baltimore, Maryland—1817

Sunlight glinted on the white-capped waves in glittering chips, and a strong northwest wind pushed the graceful two-masted vessel closer to the Maryland coast, bellying the huge white sails into smiles. It would be just past noon when the *Tempest* docked in Baltimore, and the glad cries of the crew clinging to masts and rigging could be heard among the piercing screeches of the seagulls swooping overhead. It had been a long journey, and their last night at sea had been spent battling heavy seas and a fusillade of rain. Passengers and crew alike would be glad to see the end of this journey from London.

Wooden decks scrubbed with sand and soap gleamed in the noonday sun, bare of the usual crowd of passengers lining the rails. Few could find the strength to venture from their cabins this morning, in spite of the promised end of their journey.

Lady Jessamy Montgomery, looking like a bright spring

1

flower in her yellow silk, was the only passenger on deck. She leaned eagerly against the smooth, polished rail, peering toward the town of Baltimore, now just a speck looming on the horizon. The words "journey's end" flashed through her mind, and she wondered where she had heard that phrase as she reflected on the future. What would she find at her journey's end?

Not normally one prone to worrying about the future, Jessamy nevertheless found it unsettling to have her future hinging upon one certain man, and that man was as yet unknown to her. Cornflower blue eyes darkened with annoyance and uncertainty. She had little difficulty facing problems with determination and perspicacity, but this particular dilemma required more than the usual amount of wit and tact. And at twenty-six, the young widow had often been required to exercise a great deal of wit and tact.

Small white teeth worried a full bottom lip as Jessamy turned into the press of the wind, blinking against the bright glare of the sun. A gloved hand reached up to hold the brim of her flat-crowned hat of jonquil silk, keeping it firmly atop her head and tilting it down to shade her eyes as she peered anxiously toward shore.

Baltimore was becoming visible, the land before her now growing recognizable as a city instead of a blur. It had been an interesting voyage once they had slipped from the Atlantic into Chesapeake Bay, rounding the finger of land that formed the eastern boundaries of Virginia, and gliding north toward Baltimore. There had been glimpses of towns, then long stretches of what appeared to be uninhabited wilderness.

Jessamy suppressed a shudder. Was America still an uncivilized land? She had been warned of the painted, howling savages who were said to roam the forests, but nothing could sway her determination once she was set upon a course of action. Her small chin lifted firmly, and she gave an imaginary squaring of her shoulders. She had decided what should be done, and she would do it.

"Having second thoughts?" a familiar feminine voice asked, and Jessamy turned with a smile.

"No. Are you?"

Margaret Middleton, Jessamy's nurse when she was just a motherless child, answered with asperity, "After all I've heard, anyone with a grain of common sense would have second thoughts!"

"And what have you heard, Margaret? Mind," she added, "I don't care to listen to idle gossip."

Margaret sniffed and tied the strings to her bonnet even tighter to keep it from sailing away with the wind. "It wasn't so idle," she said, tucking stray wisps of gray hair beneath the bonnet. "The cook was preparing an unsavory stew the entire time he regaled me with tales of terror concerning not only America, but our host."

"Granted our host owns this vessel, but I find it difficult to believe that a common cook would take it upon himself to gossip about his employer," Jessamy said with a note of severity in her voice.

Margaret nodded. "Well, it wasn't so much gossip as it was a tirade against 'uppity Britishers comin' over to lord it over th' rustics,' as the cook had the nerve to say . . ."

"Margaret—what did you say to the cook to provoke such an outburst?"

Hesitating, the older woman drew herself up into a quivering knot of affronted dignity. "Lady Jessamy, you know how concerned I've been over Chastity's tendency to refuse her food—your daughter's so like you at that age—

and I simply couldn't bear the thought of her having to suffer through another one of those dreadful meals the ship's cook has the effrontery to deem decent food, so I took it upon myself to confront the man . . .''

"You didn't," Jessamy said faintly, but Margaret nodded.

"I did. Of course, the crude individual resented my interference, as persons of that quality often do, and he referred to my concern as an intrusion—'butting in' was his exact phrase—so I found myself completely unwelcome."

"How dreadful," Jessamy murmured, biting back a smile at the mental picture of her old nurse visiting a ship's galley in order to procure tasty treats for her five-year-old charge. It was so like Margaret. "And then what happened?" Jessamy prompted. "Did you wish him to Jericho?"

"Well! The ridiculous man informed me that I was a hysterical British busybody who had no more business in America than I did in his galley. He also said quite snippily that this Rand Montgomery would be quick to set us right in our place—back in England."

"The horrid gargoyle," Jessamy replied sympathetically, though her private thoughts ran much along the same line. Sighing, the elegant young widow reflected that this might very well be the case. Even her own solicitor had pointed out the shortcomings in her plan, had emphasized that Rand Montgomery was said to be a man who disliked pretense and formality. He had the reputation of being a strong individual who preferred plain speaking to tact, and open confrontations to polite machinations. Could she manage such a man?

Jessamy became aware of Margaret's steady regard fixed upon her and asked politely, "What do you think about my plans, Margaret?"

"I think that you are quite capable of managing most men, my dear, but this new earl may be an exception."

"Why do you say that?"

"Perhaps he is not the country bumpkin we once thought him," was the slow reply. "It could be that our 'country cousin' is a man well acquainted with ladies' efforts to be charming."

"If that is so," Jessamy said thoughtfully, "then he should be delighted that we are visiting him. After all, how could he not enjoy the company of a cousin by marriage who has come all this way just to flatter him with a visit? I daresay, he will be, at the very least, curious."

"I daresay," Margaret agreed, gazing fondly at Jessamy. She had turned out to be a young woman of exceptional beauty, and Margaret had no doubts that the new earl would be quite enchanted with his cousin's widow. What man wouldn't be? And it wasn't just because she had been both mother and nurse to Jessamy since she was Chastity's age that she considered her beyond reproach, Margaret told herself. All who met Jessamy fell under her spell. But Jessamy had been as elusive as a spring butterfly since the death of her young husband, Jamie Montgomery, in the recent conflict between America and England.

There were times when Margaret wondered if Jessamy's devotion to her late husband's family hadn't been inspired by her own father, who had never recovered from his wife's death due to a tragic fall when Jessamy was only five years old. Sir Geoffrey Connor had grieved his lost wife until his own death several years ago. Of course, losing her husband and her father within a few months of one another had been a tragedy few young women could endure well, but Jessamy had endured with a poise and sad acceptance that made

Margaret doubly proud of her. And Jessamy had steadfastly refused to consider remarriage.

Yet perhaps it was not so much grief as devotion to Jamie's family that held her back. The Montgomerys had gladly accepted dowerless Jessamy Connor as a bride to their son—not a common practice among the aristocratic class. The marriage agreement had been based not upon youthful love between Jessamy and Jamie, but upon a filial affection between Jamie's father, the Earl of Wemyess, and Sir Geoffrey. In light of Jessamy's devotion, it had been extremely difficult for her to accept the fact that the old earl had willed his estates to Rand Montgomery instead of his granddaughter, Chastity. Kenilworth would go to a complete stranger.

"You've become terribly quiet, my lady," Margaret observed finally. "Try not to worry about the new earl."

"It's just that . . . that I wonder if he will be devilishly difficult about all this! He shouldn't be. After all, he's never even seen Kenilworth, and Chastity was born there. Oh, if only the old earl had not been so plump on protocol! Then Chastity would have her proper inheritance . . ." Jessamy paused, then added more confidently, "I will regain Kenilworth for my daughter before I leave the shores of America, Margaret."

Gazing at Jessamy, Margaret could not disagree. Not many men could refuse the winsome Lady Jessamy Montgomery anything she desired, even a gentleman with so redoubtable a reputation as the new Earl of Wemyess.

"I hope you're correct in this matter," Margaret said.

Jessamy smiled and tugged at her pale yellow gloves, pulling them more snugly over delicate, ringless fingers. "I am, Margaret. Now please inform the others that we will soon be disembarking. Oh, and ask Charles to come to me at once.''

"Certainly," Margaret replied, once more tying the strings of her fashionable blue bonnet. It had been a gift from Jessamy, and she cherished it even more for that reason. Smiling, Margaret moved across the deck with that peculiar crablike gait of a person unaccustomed to the lurch of a ship.

A few minutes went by before a tall, middle-aged man crossed the heaving deck to stand before Jessamy. "Did you ask for me, my lady?" he intoned.

"Yes, I did, Charles." Jessamy turned away from her contemplation of the crowded pier now within clear view. "I should like for Nellie, Sara, and Imogene to ride in the same carriage with Molly and Drucilla. The men may ride with you in the same carriage as the baggage."

"Of course, my lady. Will Margaret and Miss Chastity be riding with you?"

"Oh yes."

"I will see to all the arrangements once we dock, then. I presume the earl will have sent transportation?"

"Oh, certainly. I'm sure he will." Jessamy's mouth curved into a mischievous smile. "But I'm equally certain he will not have sent enough carriages for my retinue and baggage. A rustic such as the new earl will have no idea of the proper amount of baggage a lady must carry, no idea at all . . .''

Jessamy was proven correct in her assumption that the new Earl of Wemyess would not send enough carriages, but even she was aghast to discover that he had sent only one.

7

"One carriage for all of this?" Margaret moaned. "Whatever shall we do?"

As usual, Jessamy took control of the situation. "Why, we shall simply engage a few more carriages, that is what we shall do, Margaret. Don't go into a tizzy; you know it makes you ill to become too excited. Charles," she added to the patiently waiting servant who had been her late husband's personal valet, "please be so good as to procure us three more carriages." Then, turning to her young daughter who waited with perfect confidence in her mother's abilities, Jessamy smiled and said, "We're off, pet!"

The fully loaded carriage proceeded through the narrow streets of Baltimore at a slow, deliberate pace that prompted Jessamy to order the coachman to increase his speed. It did not pass her notice that on more than one occasion he would mutter some tart rebuttal concerning his skill and her femininity, all of which she ignored.

"Baltimore is big, Mama," Chastity said, staring with wide eyes at the brick buildings they passed. "How big is it?"

"I believe the captain of the *Tempest* said it was a city of close to thirty thousand people, pet," Jessamy replied. "Baltimore is the second largest seaport in the United States, and as you have seen, one of the busiest."

Chastity, with pale hair the color of corn silk and wide blue eyes very much like her mother's, nodded wisely. "Yes, it *was* quite busy, wasn't it. I think it is a very pretty place, though, with all the trees and these fresh-painted houses. Don't you, Miss Middleton?"

"Yes indeed, my little poppet," Margaret answered, gripping the side of the open carriage with one hand as they turned a corner. "Very pretty."

When they finally reached the large Georgian brick home

that was their destination, the footman managed to have the door of the carriage open before the horses had come to a complete stop.

"My word!" Margaret gasped, "I do hope the rest of our visit is not so trying. I thought we would never arrive, and now that we have, we're being rushed out of our conveyance before it comes to a halt . . ."

Before Jessamy had a chance to vent similar feelings, the footman had the steps down and was helping Chastity from the carriage. Jessamy stared at him for several moments, fascinated by his appearance. He was dressed impeccably, with a frogged uniform and gleaming shoes that were almost as shiny as his bald head. What fascinated her the most was the color of his skin, for he was the deep, rich color of coffee, and when he smiled his teeth were blinding white.

"How unusual," she murmured, and the footman turned to her.

"Did you say sumthin', ma'am?" he asked politely, obviously trying to give her the closest attention.

Masking her surprise that a footman would speak to her without having been directly addressed, Jessamy answered, "Why . . . yes, I was remarking upon how quickly we have been attended, and . . ."—she paused as she was handed down from the carriage—"how . . . *cautiously* . . . we were brought from the dock."

White teeth flashed brilliantly. "Yes'm, that do be true, ah'm sure! Boris surely does drive fast . . . plumb reckless at times . . . tryin' ta get Mistah Rand here and there when he wants. But Mistah Rand now, he done scolded Boris 'bout that, and said as how there better be no racin' with you and yore chile. He was ta drive that carriage lak it was movin' along on eggshells, real s . . . l . . . o . . . w. And he told me I's better not keep you English ladies waitin' since you be used to peoples waitin' on yore ev'ry need."

"He said that, did he?" Jessamy remarked with a chilly smile. "How *kind* of 'Mister Rand' to be so solicitous of our welfare."

It was quite simple to read between the lines. The new earl obviously considered his guests to be nuisances, and pampered females. "Is the earl in residence?" she asked the garrulous footman.

"Oh no, ma'am. He done gone over ta Miss Selma's house ta see 'bout buyin' her prize hawg." His grin widened even further, a feat Jessamy had imagined to be impossible. "That pig be the biggest hawg I ever laid eyes on, and shore ta be good eatin'. Mistah Rand gonna have that hawg cooked for the picnic he's plannin' in a few weeks."

"Merciful heavens," Margaret murmured as she descended from the carriage to take Chastity in her arms. "Why are we standing upon the steps conversing with a footman about ...pigs, Lady Jessamy? Shouldn't we be shown into the house and at least be presented to the *housekeeper* if our host is unavailable? This is not at all proper, not at all."

"Yes, Margaret," Jessamy soothed, "I realize that. But we are in America, remember? Perhaps this is a less ...*formal* country than England."

"I should say so!" her old nurse exclaimed indignantly, then muttered in an undertone as she lifted the hem of her skirts to keep them from dusting the walkway. "Conversing with a *footman* of all things! And about *pigs*!"

The housekeeper, Jessamy and Margaret discovered, was one and the same as the footman.

"*You* are the housekeeper?" Jessamy echoed, staring at

the dusky face of the man she had thought the footman. "Is there a shortage of servants in America?"

"Oh no, ma'am," the footman, whose name was William, replied. "Mistah Rand jus' don' lak a lot of people 'round him too much. He says we kin git along jus' fine without 'em."

"I see," Jessamy lied politely. "How quaint..."

"We done got yore room ready upstairs, and one downstairs in th' servants' quarters for yore maid..."

"I'm the child's nurse," Margaret interrupted sternly, "*not* a maid!"

"Yas'm. Anyhow, we readied two rooms..."

"Only two?" Jessamy burst out, feeling slightly ill. "That will never do, William. There are six men waiting at the dock with my baggage, and I have several servants traveling with me also."

A frown creased his forehead as William considered this startling news. "Well now, Mistah Rand shore gonna be surprised at all you people in his house, but ah'll see what I kin do."

"Please do so as soon as possible," Jessamy said firmly, stifling the irritation she felt. The Earl of Wemyess must be a complete provincial if he didn't realize that a lady must be accompanied by an entourage of personal servants, especially across so great a distance as this journey had been! "I must have a room for myself, and my daughter and her nurse, my personal cook Nellie, and my maids, Imogene, Molly, Sara, and Drucilla must all have rooms. I also brought along my late husband's personal valet and my own footmen."

"Oh me," William moaned, "Mistah Rand ain't gonna lak this at all..."

"Life is filled with disappointments," Jessamy returned

promptly. "He will simply have to grow accustomed to it."

Margaret eyed Jessamy narrowly. There was a note in her voice that indicated enjoyment of the inconvenience she was causing her "country cousin." Not that she, Margaret, wasn't the tiniest bit glad that the new earl would be discomposed. After all, the recent conflict between England and America had left both nations with a certain amount of bitterness. In this case, the British would have another opportunity to tweak the nose of a colonial rebel.

✳ Chapter 2 ✳

Though the house was much smaller than those Jessamy was accustomed to in England, it was quite nice, even elegant. The large drawing room of the Baltimore house boasted doors, long windows, and cornices that had been designed and carved with classical styling. Window curtains and wall hangings were fashioned of gold-fringed satin damask, decorated with a lovely design of serpentine ribands and large sprays of gold flowers on a background of blue and cream. There were two classical sculptures, one of the Greek Epictetus, and another of the fiery Frenchman Voltaire, placed between the long windows. Carpets were of a rich, fine texture in the popular Pompeiian style, while the wallpaper had obviously been hand painted in France.

Jessamy's gaze drifted gloomily around the room. Shallow pilasters enriched with stucco arabesques divided the walls into sections niched for statues and recessed bookcases, and the panels were framed by light moldings. It was not, Jessamy decided, the abode of a clumsy country bumpkin. Could it be that her late husband's cousin possessed good taste? That notion was quite disturbing.

Jessamy's reverie was interrupted by a polite "harrumph" from William, the footman/housekeeper. Turning, she arched a delicate brow and said, "Yes?"

"Your rooms are almost ready, ma'am. Would you lak some refreshments?"

Tugging off her gloves, Jessamy nodded. "That would be lovely."

"I'll have Bessie—she's our cook—fix you ladies some tall glasses of lemonade, then."

"Lemonade?" Margaret echoed faintly, exchanging glances with Jessamy. "We had in mind . . . perhaps . . . would a nice pot of tea be out of the question?"

"Tea?" William gazed at them for a moment, then shook his head. "Tea kin be fixed, I reckon." He paused. "Would you be wantin' *hot* tea, ma'am?"

"Well, of course. What other kind do you have?" Margaret asked, then held up her hand palm outward. "Never mind," she added. "Just bring us hot tea and three cups, please."

"I'd like some lemonade," Chastity offered, and William broke into a smile.

"Of course, little missy! You kin have ennything you want. Jus' ask ole Wills, and ah'll git it fer you . . ."

"Ole Wills?" Chastity looked up and smiled. "Is that you?"

"Yes, ma'am, little missy! It shore is, and ah'll be right back with some lemonade and . . . hot tea," he promised, bowing as correctly as any proper English servant before he left the drawing room.

Jessamy placed her gloves on a small lamp table and sank into the comfort of a plush brocade settee, removing her hat with careless grace. "Perhaps Chastity should go up to her room after she has her lemonade, Margaret. I'm certain she will need to rest before dinner, and I intend to do the same."

"Of course. We could all do with some rest," Margaret replied, glancing around the drawing room. "I just wonder if there will be room in this house for all of us."

"Oh, I am certain the earl will find nooks and crannies that will stow us all safely from his sight," Jessamy said tartly. "He may display a certain amount of taste with his elegantly decorated home, but he sounds rather like a muttonheaded swell who cares little for those around him."

"Do you think so?" Margaret murmured thoughtfully. "His servant certainly seems to admire his master."

Jessamy shot her old nurse a skeptical glance. "I daresay he is just grateful for his position, though I cannot imagine why, what with the obvious shortage of proper servants in America."

Sighing, Margaret took a seat upon a tufted chair crafted by Chippendale and smoothed her taffeta skirts. "I do think the earl might just be thrifty . . ."

"Another term for stingy," Jessamy sniffed, taking an unconscionable dislike to the unknown earl. Of course, to be fair, she would have to admit that she had disliked him immediately upon hearing that it was he who had inherited Kenilworth instead of Chastity. But since no one had yet asked her about it, she would just keep that information to herself.

"And he does have good taste," Margaret offered in defense of the absent earl.

Jessamy dismissed that excuse with, "He hired a decorator, of course."

Margaret leveled a severe stare at Jessamy. "Where's your sense of justice?"

"Where was the earl's when he casually accepted lands he didn't care about and had never seen? Surely he received my letters asking him to relinquish his hold on estates he would never see!" Jessamy leaped up from the settee and began pacing the carpet in tight circles, clearly agitated. "This entire journey could have been avoided if he had only heeded my pleas and allowed Chastity to inherit the lands her father had loved . . ."

Drawing herself up, Margaret reminded gently, "But the old earl himself left the estates to this Rand Montgomery, my dear. Have you forgotten?"

Jessamy pressed her fingers to her brow and closed her eyes. "No, but I do not think that he was aware of what he was doing when he concocted that will, Margaret, or he would have . . ."

"Done exactly as he did," Margaret finished for her. "I really think he would have, Jessamy. After all, he was very conscious of lineage and protocol."

"Hang lineage and protocol!" Jessamy said fiercely, whirling to face Margaret. "I intend to coax this new earl into giving my daughter her rightful inheritance by hook or crook . . ."

Fortunately, the arrival of a silver tray interrupted a further diatribe on the new earl and his misbegotten inheritance. Calming herself, Jessamy poured the tea while Margaret helped Chastity with her glass of lemonade. Small cakes and dainty pastries accompanied the drinks, which proved to Margaret that Americans had *some* notion of how to serve proper refreshment, if not the correct one. Of course, tea was not usually served until four o'clock, but as they were weary and the ride from the dock had been undertaken in such a haphazard manner—finding the proper vehicle and ascertaining that the coachman was, indeed, sent from Mister Rand Montgomery expressly for the purpose of conveying the ladies to his home—these refreshments were most welcome an hour early.

Chastity was yawning widely by the time her glass of lemonade was empty, tempting Jessamy and Margaret to be quite rude and do the same.

"I'll take her up now," Margaret said, gathering the sleepy child into her arms. "I believe that Charles and the others have finally arrived from the dock, so Nellie can assist you with your baggage."

"Thank you, Margaret," Jessamy murmured, and when their eyes met the old nurse smiled.

"Of course, my dear. I always understand. You have been under too much strain lately, and I will be just as pleased as you when this is over."

Jessamy's answering smile revealed her fatigue, and she pulled at a stray wisp of pale blond hair with the same gesture she had used when she was a small, weary child. "I almost wish you could put me to bed again as you do Chastity," she said.

"You never did care for my lullabyes," Margaret returned, and Jessamy laughed.

"It wasn't the lullabyes, it was your singing voice," she said. "I recall telling you that you sounded rather like a rusty wheel..."

"And you were right," Margaret admitted ruefully. "Rest now, my dear, and I will see you later this evening."

Jessamy was still smiling when she went into the entrance hall to greet her entourage and give them their instructions on where to put the baggage.

* * *

Opening the front door of his comfortable home, Rand Montgomery stopped dead in his tracks, gazing with considerable awe at what appeared to be a country fair. There were unfamiliar faces bustling busily about from room to room, and piles of baggage littered the marble floor of his small entrance hall, obliterating his view of any portion of the walls. There were crates and cartons, leather bags and cotton sacks, books, a fascinating assortment of toys, and various feminine articles scattered about.

Swallowing his irritation, Rand plowed his way through the maze of boxed goods and climbed the curved stairway with great determination. His resoluteness suffered a slight setback when he arrived at the top of the stairs and discovered that the second-floor landing was equally as cluttered. Scowling, Rand surveyed bannisters and doors draped with gaily colored gowns. There were morning gowns, riding habits, ball gowns, gowns for teas, for carriage rides, for walking, and for dining. Streamers of lace and trims decorated any empty surface that could be found, and there were countless pairs of shoes and gloves lying about while various maids sorted them with great concentration. There were painted fans, sheer silk stockings, beaded reticules, and an entire box of cashmere shawls.

For one mad moment, Rand thought that he must have stumbled into the midst of a bazaar. Reaching down, he lifted a stylish chipped-straw bonnet trimmed with tiny pink flowers. What kind of woman wore such a thing? he was musing when William found him.

"Mistah Rand! Izzat you? Oh lawdy, you done got home and seen all this trampin'!"

"Is that what this is?" Rand asked abruptly. He deposited the bonnet back in its place, on the bust of Socrates that usually sat in dignified solitude upon the small table now decorated with frills.

"Yassah, it's yore English ladies. They done arrived, and this here is all their clothes and such." William paused, gazing skeptically at the piles of garments. "I been tryin', but I don't know that there's enough room in all of Baltimore for all these trampin's!"

"I daresay you're quite right about that," Rand returned coolly. "Shall I send for the ragpicker to assist them?"

Flustered, William just stared at his employer for a moment, and was relieved to see the beginning of a smile in Rand's eyes, thawing some of the ice. "He don't have a big enough wagon," William said, and Rand grinned.

"I believe you're right. Where is the young lady who has wrecked my home when all of her fellow countrymen could not? Amazing, isn't it? Baltimore is almost burned to the ground by the British, yet my house remained intact. Now, one simple visit from this British bombshell, and my house is in chaos . . ."

William coughed politely, then said, "The young lady is napping, Mistah Rand, and so is her chile. They wanted to rest before supper."

"Supper . . . Good God! She won't bring a small child to my table, I hope! That would be a disaster," Rand observed.

"I dunno, Mistah Rand, but she did bring her own cook," William offered.

Dark brows arched high. Leaning against a doorjamb as he contemplated the confusion in his hall and his servant's carefully impassive face, Rand shrugged his broad shoulders in resignation. "And a small army as well, it seems. How many servants did she bring?"

William begin ticking them off on his fingers, ending with, "And a nurse for the little girl."

"And a partridge in a pear tree?" Rand snapped sarcastically. Shoving away from the doorjamb, he impatiently tapped his riding crop against a lean muscled thigh clad in form-fitting fawn trousers as he reflected upon the foolishness of allowing distant relatives to descend upon one's home. His expertly tied cravat would have given any London dandy a flush of pride, and the shoulders of his pale blue coat needed no padding at all. Dark hair was tossed in casual waves upon his high forehead, and sensual lips tightened into a grimace.

"Clear me a path to my bedchamber, Wills," he ordered, adding, "I *do* still have my bedchamber?"

Bobbing his close-cropped head, William said hastily, "Yassuh, yassuh! Of course you do! And thar ain't no petticoats in it, neither!"

"I suppose," the new earl said slowly, "that I am intended to draw some sort of satisfaction from that, William, but somehow I find it most difficult."

Ducking, he managed to avoid collision with a gown of Italian green taffeta as he entered his rooms, swearing lightly under his breath. Supper should be quite an entertaining diversion on this particular evening, he decided, quite entertaining.

At precisely a quarter past seven of the clock that evening, Lady Jessamy Daphne Connor Montgomery sailed into the brilliantly lit dining room with all the graceful aplomb she could manage.

"Good evening, my lord," she said to the granite-faced man sitting at the far end of the long table, smiling her most winsome smile.

There was no answering smile as the new earl remained

seated and said quite coolly, "Good evening, Lady Montgomery."

William, who apparently also served as footman at the side table of serving dishes, swiftly and efficiently pulled out Jessamy's chair to seat her. She took her place, eyes drawn to the far end of the table where the earl sat in forbidding silence. Candlelight from the chandelier and the seven—she counted them—silver candelabras on the table flickered across Rand Montgomery's face. Jessamy suppressed a shiver of foreboding. She had not expected him to be overcome with rapture upon seeing her, but neither had she expected this hostile rudeness. And, if the truth were known, she had not expected the new earl to be quite so handsome, either.

Aping his aloof attitude, Jessamy nodded her head in her most regal manner, and took scant comfort in the fact that she had taken great pains to look her best this evening, and had succeeded. Her hair had been drawn up into loose curls atop her head, delicately framing her oval face, and the cheval mirror in her bedchamber—swept free of laces and scarves—had shown her to be dressed to the nines.

The deep rich blue of her crepe gown brought out the blue in her eyes to great advantage, and the front, which opened over a slip of white satin, was ornamented with clasps of tiny white roses to match the posies artfully placed among her shining blond curls. She had chosen to wear almost no jewelry, only slipping on a strand of exquisitely matched pearls that shone with a dull luster around her neck. White satin slippers had completed the effort, and Jessamy was well aware that she looked her absolute best, a fact which the earl noted rather grudgingly, she thought.

"Considering the . . . confusion . . . upstairs, madam, you

seem to have managed to attire yourself quite charmingly,"
he said after those first few moments of appraising silence.

Was she supposed to *thank* him for that compliment?
Jessamy seethed silently, but smiled as warmly as if he had
compared her to Venus.

"Indeed, my lord? I am delighted that you noticed," she
said, long lashes lowering to hide any telltale fires of pique
in her eyes. Even though he sat so far away, it would not do
to take chances at this early stage in the game. Jessamy
suffered a brief regret that she must appear to be a simpering
idiot in order to further her ends, then glanced up at the earl
with what she hoped was an admiring smile.

Deciding that a subtle set-down could not hurt, Jessamy
continued in the same softly interested tone, "I had not
heard about your injury, my lord. I do hope it's not
permanent?"

"Injury?" Rand echoed, frowning. One finger rose to
trace the long, jagged scar that marred the smooth perfec-
tion of his face, and Jessamy was appalled that she had not
noticed it before.

"I mean . . your . . . your *leg* injury, my lord," she said
quickly, thinking that the scar along his jawline did not
detract from his rugged good looks in the least.

"I have no idea what you're talking about," the earl said
abruptly.

Jessamy fluttered in pretty confusion, "Oh well, since
you did not rise when I entered I just assumed . . . well, you
know that most gentlemen—unless they are injured, of
course—always rise when a lady enters the room, and I just
supposed that . . . that . . ."

"That I must be crippled? Or have a wooden leg?" Rand
finished for her. A slow smile slanted his mouth as he
considered the woman opposite him. He had noticed the

tiny fires of rebellion in her eyes and had seen the unconscious set of her chin at his obvious rudeness. The role of mindless coquette was not a part familiar to her, he saw at once, so he decided to end their light sparring. After all, he had discovered what he'd wanted to know about the young lady, and was not unpleasantly surprised.

"I am not crippled, nor do I have a wooden leg," Rand said smoothly. "I was being purposely rude."

Jessamy stared at him. Slender fingers curled around the stem of her water glass as she quickly discarded several impetuous remarks and said instead, "Oh? And why did you feel that you must be rude to me, my lord?"

Leaning forward so that his deep, dark eyes met hers, Rand said softly, "I felt it necessary to chastise you for creating chaos in my normally peaceful home, Lady Jessamy. I can now see that you did not intend to do so, but that this is merely your customary style of traveling."

Sensing that this was as near to an apology as he would come, Jessamy decided to let bygones be bygones. "I apologize for any inconvenience you have suffered by my presence," she said. "I had not considered that space would be so . . . limited." In spite of her irritation and animosity, she could not help but feel a certain admiration for the earl when he smiled so charmingly. It changed his appearance entirely.

"Perhaps we should begin again?" Rand suggested, and Jessamy nodded.

"That would be quite nice, my lord."

"Please—do not refer to me as 'my lord,'" he protested. "I find myself quite uncomfortable with that title, and as you may have heard, Americans prefer to be addressed more informally."

"Certainly, my . . . Mister Montgomery. I will try to oblige you," Jessamy said, "though it will seem quite unnatural to me." If the new earl disavowed even the title, then would he not be easier to persuade into relinquishing the estates? she wondered. She let her gaze travel over his face, lingering for a moment on the scar along his left jawline, then moving over his high cheekbones and fine, deep eyes, the straight nose and firmly chiseled lips. Rand Montgomery was a most attractive man.

"Lady Jessamy?" a voice said at her elbow, startling her from her contemplation of the man she considered her opponent, and she looked up to see William. "I didn't want to spill the hot soup on yore dress," he apologized, setting down a china bowl of thin, clear broth.

Rather embarrassed that she had been caught "out," Jessamy just nodded as William arranged the bowl with white-gloved hands. The dinner courses followed one another swiftly, and to her surprise, Jessamy was unable to summon much of an appetite. Perhaps it was all the excitement, the arrival in an unfamiliar land with a pocketful of hopes that might never materialize; whatever the reason, she only nibbled daintily at her food.

Finally dinner was over, the dishes had been quietly and efficiently removed, and sherry offered to Jessamy.

"Shall we take our after-dinner glasses into the small parlor?" Rand suggested, and she fell in with this idea eagerly.

As tired as she was, Jessamy deemed it most important to try to discover exactly what Mr. Montgomery might have in mind concerning his late cousin's widow.

"I understand your daughter is with you," Rand said politely when they were comfortably installed in the small parlor. "And what is her age?"

"She is five years old," Jessamy replied, "and a most

delightful child. I am quite certain you will be enchanted by Chastity. Everyone who meets her falls under her spell.''

In Rand's experience, most mothers thought their children delightful in spite of the fact that the little beasts terrorized their nurses and wantonly destroyed whatever took their fancy, so he wisely remained silent on that particular subject, commenting instead, ''Was your voyage uneventful?''

''Yes, but for a sudden squall or two that made us all green and longing for solid land beneath our feet.'' She laughed, recalling the swift exodus of passengers from the dining room one particularly rough evening. ''Margaret claims I was blessed with a cast-iron stomach,'' she explained when Rand cocked an inquiring brow in her direction. ''I didn't experience a moment's discomfort the entire voyage.''

''A born sailor,'' Rand said with a smile.

''No, Jamie was the sailor in the family. I prefer dry land beneath me.'' Jessamy paused to take a sip of excellent sherry from the tiny glass she held. Lamplight softened the pale blond of her hair to silver, and her long lashes cast deep shadows upon her cheeks.

''I regret I never had the opportunity to know my cousin,'' Rand said then. ''We were, by circumstance and birth, on opposing sides during the recent conflict, of course, but I still would like to have known my kinsman.''

''He was killed in Maryland,'' Jessamy said, and set down her glass upon the lamp table, missing Rand's soft murmur of affirmation as she did so. Rising abruptly from her chair, she stepped to the marble fireplace, where a small fire burned brightly, struggling against conflicting emotions. The war between America and England was over and should be buried, but so many had been lost, and there was still so much bitterness between the nations at times.

"It is best forgotten," Rand said then. "I do my best to erase it from my memory." Strong fingers curved around his snifter of brandy as he levelled a long gaze at his guest. "Much was lost on both sides."

"Yes," she murmured. "It was. Shall we do our part to patch things up between America and Britain, Mr. Montgomery?"

He smiled, his eyes crinkling at the corners and his lips slanting most attractively, Jessamy thought. "I think that is an excellent notion, Lady Montgomery. And since we are cousins, why don't we be less formal? Call me Rand, please."

Hesitating a moment, Jessamy considered his suggestion. Perhaps if she were on more familiar terms with him, she could more easily appeal to his better nature—assuming he had one.

"Of course, Rand. And you must address me as Jessamy. I think we shall get along splendidly, just splendidly." Her smile was bright, but somewhere in the back of her mind she could not help but recall the stone-faced man who had confronted her when she first walked into the dining room. Rand Montgomery was a complex man, and definitely not the country bumpkin she had once thought him. It would not do to underestimate him in spite of their outward show of affability; no, it would not do at all.

Moving to retrieve her fragile glass of sherry, Jessamy held it up and proposed a toast. "To friendship," she said, and Rand smiled more widely, inclining his head and parroting her words.

"To friendship," he said, gazing over the brim of his snifter at Jessamy.

✳ Chapter 3 ✳

Jessamy awoke the next morning feeling fully relaxed after the long ocean voyage and her arrival in Baltimore. Sitting up in bed, she gazed about the comfortably furnished bedchamber. It was much smaller than any of those at Kenilworth, yet it was equally as elegant.

A drift of gauze canopy one of the maids had identified as mosquito netting wafted in gentle folds around the four posts of the delicately carved rice bed. A coverlet of blue floral print was neatly folded over a blanket rack at the end of the bed, and sweet-smelling sheets lay in soft folds upon the mattress. A carved washstand stood nearby, bearing a cake of lavender-scented soap and a brimming pitcher of water for her morning ablutions. The earl's staff, though small, was quite efficient.

Yawning, Jessamy eased from the bed and posed in a very unladylike stretch, her thin lawn gown shifting around her ankles in tickling swirls. It wouldn't do to be late for breakfast her first morning in America.

Imogene and Sara had Jessamy dressed and ready in very

27

short order, garbing her in a simple gown of flowing ivory muslin that made her pale English complexion seem even more attractive than usual. The short, puffed sleeves and scooped bodice lay bare a gleaming expanse of creamy skin decorated with only a single, shimmering pendant. The sapphire stone reflected with the same blue as her eyes.

"You look quite lovely, my lady," Sara said truthfully, bobbing her mistress a curtsy. "The earl should be impressed."

"Somehow I doubt that," Jessamy returned dryly, "but thank you, Sara. I am ready to beard the lion in his den!"

Rand was sitting in the cozy, sunlit breakfast room when Jessamy strolled in with a bright smile. He rose to his feet as she entered and gave a polite bow.

"Good morning," she said cheerfully, flashing William a smile also as he seated her.

"Good morning," Rand returned, eyeing her with a wary smile as he sat back down. "You certainly seem well rested."

"I am. And I am also starving."

"Does your daughter plan to join us this morning?" Rand asked politely.

"No, Margaret, her nurse, is letting her take breakfast in her room. The poor child is still weary from our long journey."

Uttering a silent prayer of gratitude for small favors, Rand smiled more genuinely as he observed Jessamy. She seemed so fragile, like a bright summer butterfly who had paused for a moment to sip nectar from a delicate blossom before flitting past with a flutter of fragile wings.

But as Jessamy devoured several eggs, three thick slices of Virginia ham, two blueberry muffins, four biscuits laden with blackberry jam and apple butter, and a generous helping of fried potatoes and onions, Rand began to change his mind about his ill-chosen metaphor. Perhaps she should be compared to a ravenous wolverine instead of a butterfly, he mused, watching with astonishment as she finished off a large slice of beef.

"Delicious," she said, daintily patting her mouth with the edge of her linen napkin. "I have never tasted food prepared in quite this manner. I find it surprisingly good."

"Apparently so," Rand muttered, wondering if she would be able to rise from her chair. "Is that why you brought your own cook?" he asked after a moment.

"Yes. I must admit to a bit of apprehension concerning American food. This, however, was most pleasing."

"Your Nellie said the same thing."

"You met her?" Jessamy asked in astonishment. "Where?"

"In the kitchen, of course. I convinced her to let you at least try a few of our dishes before she began turning my kitchen upside down."

"How foresighted," Jessamy murmured.

"Yes, wasn't it?" Rand's fingers drummed against the tabletop as he regarded his guest with a smile.

Blue eyes narrowed as Jessamy forced an answering smile. This provincial American was beginning to get on her nerves. Was it because of her appetite, perhaps, that he was staring at her so oddly?

"Pardon my manners if I seem to have been unusually hungry," she excused herself, "but I have never been one to pick daintily at my food. I consider it an insult to both host and cook, and I enjoy eating too much to pretend indifference. I just eat and eat and never seem to become too full or portly..." She paused, cheeks flushing as she realized how she was rambling. "I'm sorry... have I talked too much?" she asked, placing her fork across the plate.

"No, not at all. I admire a woman who can speak her mind—regardless of the subject."

Jessamy's brow arched delicately at the odd note in his voice. "Would you prefer a loftier subject, my lord?"

Tensing, Rand regarded her for a moment with a distinctly dissatisfied expression in his dark eyes. "I would appreciate it, Lady Jessamy, if you would refrain from addressing me as anything but 'mister'."

"I apologize," she returned stiffly.

"Tut, tut. No need for an apology. Just remember in the future that this is America. We have no royalty here."

"I understand," she said lightly. "I thought for a moment there that you objected to my appetite, not my manners." She sipped at her tea, peering at him over the thin rim of her cup.

"Oh, I see. But you misunderstand," Rand assured her with a sly twinkle in his dark eyes. "I was just surprised at your . . . endurance."

Slanting him a narrow glance, Jessamy took another sip of the hot tea provided by William before she replied, "I have a great deal of endurance, you will find."

"I am certain of that," was Rand's immediate response. He regarded her gravely, his face in shadow because of the morning sun at his back. The muted clatter of china as William gathered the soiled dishes provided the only sounds in the breakfast room for several moments, until Rand cleared his throat and said, "And now, if you will be so kind as to excuse me, I must take my leave."

Jessamy was, for some illogical reason, admiring the slant of sunshine glittering in his dark hair with warm lights, so that his meaning escaped her until he slid back his chair and rose from the table.

"You're leaving?" she asked.

One side of his mouth slanted upward. "Yes, I'm afraid so. It's been most delightful, Lady Jessamy, but I must attend to business."

Hastily scraping back her chair, Jessamy rose also, feeling more comfortable standing. He was so tall that she felt at a definite disadvantage remaining seated.

"I was hoping you might have a few moments to meet Jamie's daughter," she said lightly.

"I have already met the young lady in passing," Rand said evasively, earning a sharp glance from Jessamy.

She had planned a special introduction to Chastity, an introduction that would have suited her plans for regaining Kenilworth. For the first time, Jessamy began to feel a decided uneasiness in the presence of this most unpredictable man. Had she really been so naïve as to think she could simply charm him? Now she realized that he was a man who was not likely to lose control of a situation, and she began to wonder what had passed between Rand Montgomery and her daughter. Jessamy forced a smile and a light tone, attempting to gain some control over her own tumultuous emotions. She would not give up yet . . .

"You met Chastity? Pray, when did you meet my daughter?"

"Early this morning, when she informed me quite bluntly that I had far too small a house for an earl." Rand's smile was wry. "Of course, I forebore pointing out the fact that the house was quite large enough for me before being besieged by a plethora of British petticoats . . ."

"I admire your restraint," Jessamy said coolly. "And did you discuss any other important matters with my daughter?"

"I did, indeed, but very briefly. I suggest you speak to her if you wish to discover the nature of our conversation, because I am already running a bit behind schedule."

He bowed politely again, surprising Jessamy by reaching

out to grasp her hand in Continental fashion. "You see," he said with a twinkle in his eye, "I *do* have some notion of how to behave in society, even if it is only American society. And by the way, I have taken the liberty of arranging for you to meet Baltimore society while you are here, Lady Jessamy. I have also taken it upon myself to ascertain that you will be comfortably received. I have arranged for you to meet some of my companions and acquaintances so that you may establish yourself in society and feel at home here in America. I am certain you will enjoy all the social activities that have been planned for you," he added, "including the soirée that I have planned in a fortnight."

"You have?" Jessamy asked in surprise. She had not expected the new earl to be willing for her to mingle so freely with Baltimore society. After all, it was only 1817, and the war was still fresh in the minds of everyone, including herself. This was Maryland, the state that had suffered so much at the hands of the British. And, she thought, tensing, this was also the state that had seen her husband fall to the powder of American weapons.

Rand was looking at her closely with a strange expression in his eyes, much like a cat about to spring upon a hapless mouse. "The soirée will include only a few of my close friends, people who wish to welcome you to Baltimore and ensure that you are happily received into society," he was saying.

Jessamy managed a smile, murmuring, "That would be lovely."

"I thought you might be pleased," Rand said.

"I do hope you have not gone to too much trouble on my account," Jessamy added.

"Trouble?" Rand laughed. "What an odd word to use. You are no trouble, Lady Jessamy."

Jessamy had the distinct impression that his words and his tone were at odds. It made her uncomfortable to feel as if she was trouble, even though she did not know in what way. "I do hope you speak the truth, Mr. Montgomery. I did not come to America to place an unwelcome burden upon you."

"Not at all, my dear lady, not at all." He took her hand and lifted it to his lips, gently grazing her fingertips, his eyes lingering on her face.

Jessamy shivered, hot and cold at the same time. A rueful smile pressed at her mouth as she realized again that Rand Montgomery was not at all the country bumpkin she had once thought him.

"I shall bid you a good day now," he was saying. "Perhaps I shall see you at dinner tonight."

"Yes," she murmured. "That would be nice." Her eyes dropped to his hand where it was still gripping hers.

Rand squeezed slightly, then let his hand drop casually to his side, smiling down at her. He was so handsome, even with the deep scar running across his cheek, and it was because she was concentrating upon that that it took a moment for his words to penetrate.

"Pardon?" she asked, blinking up at him.

"I said, you will be a big success at the soirée, of that I am quite certain."

It wasn't his words but his tone that alerted her to something amiss, Jessamy realized with a frown, but all she said was, "Well, I certainly wouldn't wish to disgrace my benefactor, so I do hope all your friends approve of me."

Rand's smile faded. "I trust that you will never disgrace *me* in any way," he said in a harsh tone, leaving Jessamy to wonder why it bothered him so much to be considered her benefactor. Surely the acknowledgment of wealth and power should be pleasing to any man, but then she had learned that this was not a man who would lightly shun any sort of responsibility.

"I should not think that I would ever disgrace you, myself, my daughter, or my heritage, Mr. Montgomery," she said quietly, her chin lifting in a faintly proud gesture.

Rand's dark head inclined slightly, a smile slanting his mouth. Then he was gone, his tall frame disappearing from the breakfast room before she could speak.

This visit was not working out at all as she had planned, Jessamy thought, gazing after the earl with mixed feelings. No, not at all. What had he meant by all that?

"It's all fustian!" she said aloud, startling William.

"Did you say somethin', ma'am?" he asked, looking up from the sideboard where he was cleaning.

"No, William, I was only making an observation," she said with a tight smile. If the new Earl of Wemyess thought for one moment that she could be diverted with a few silly parties, he would soon discover that he was quite mistaken!

✳ Chapter 4 ✳

Jessamy rose early every morning for the next four days and hurried down to have breakfast with the earl. On two occasions she found an empty breakfast room, and was told that the earl had already eaten and departed.

"Oh fudge," she muttered under her breath when told one particularly bright morning that she had once again missed him, "I shall *never* have the opportunity to corner the beast!"

But the opportunity came the very next morning, when she appeared in the breakfast room determinedly early and dressed in one of her prettiest frocks, a thin muslin sprigged with tiny pink rosebuds.

"Good morning." Jessamy greeted him with her customary cheerfulness.

"Good morning," the earl returned, half-rising and glancing up from a sheaf of papers he was perusing. His glance was arrested by the pretty sight Jessamy made, and his smile grew from perfunctory to admiring. "You look very lovely today, Lady Jessamy."

"Thank you," she replied, seating herself in the chair William had pulled out for her. "Are those riding clothes you are wearing, sir?"

"You're very observant. Yes, they are," Rand said, resuming his seat. He folded his papers and put them aside. "I sometimes ride before breakfast in the mornings."

"Oh? I would often ride over the estates on my favorite mare, a real bonesetter. She has plenty of pluck, and always gives me a great go, a real runner."

He gazed at her for a moment. "You like to ride then," he said. "I have some great blood in my stables that you are welcome to try. Just ask my groom, Garfield, to assist you."

Jessamy glowed with genuine pleasure. The prospect of another long day of boredom had been quite daunting. "I most certainly will. Unoccupied days grow tedious and wearisome, I fear."

"Bored already, Lady Jessamy?" the earl asked with a slightly mocking smile. "Perhaps America is too tame for you."

"Not necessarily. Shopping is just not one of my priorities, and never has been, though I do find your shops here quite surprising."

"Even primitives offer a variety of wares, you'll find," Rand replied smoothly.

"I would hardly refer to your shops as 'primitive,'" Jessamy returned just as smoothly, wondering why even the simplest conversation with this boor degenerated into trading barbed quips. "I found a delightful assortment of ribbons and laces, materials and new patterns from France in one shop, and exquisite hats in a milliner's. No, I would hardly refer to your Baltimore shops as primitive," she concluded thoughtfully.

"Surprised?" Rand asked with the beginning of a smile pressing at his mouth. "I had the impression all British people considered Americans quite provincial."

Laughing, Jessamy teased, "Well, I won't argue that point, but to answer your question—yes, I *am* surprised. I had not thought America would be this civilized. I mean, after hearing about the savages still roaming your forests, I really didn't know quite what to expect."

"Yet you still dared those dangers to come for a friendly visit," Rand commented suavely. "How very adventurous of you, cousin."

Jessamy's cheeks flushed rosy, and her chin lifted in that faint, defiant tilt Rand had begun to recognize. "One must take chances in life in order to gain any—experience," she replied. "Don't you think?"

"Indeed I do. Just what type of 'experience' are you searching, Lady Jessamy?"

How dare he quiz her like this! Jessamy thought furiously. It was enough that she had to endure such pointed queries, but to toss them out so carelessly—when he must know what she had come for—was infuriating.

Taking a slow, deliberate sip of her hot tea, Jessamy fenced for time, then finally replied, "Since an American has inherited Kenilworth, I decided to acquaint myself with your customs. After all, I assume that some of them will be incorporated into the management of your newly acquired estates."

"And that would distress you," he said with an intuitiveness that set her teeth on edge. "I understand perfectly." He lifted one finger and William was at his side immediately, pouring him a cup of the fresh, fragrant coffee that Jessamy thought smelled so delicious and tasted so barbaric.

She took another sip of tea, narrowing her eyes at the

earl. "No, I suppose I would not really be so much upset as I would be uncomfortable." Smiling, Jessamy set her cup back in its saucer and folded both hands beneath her chin, gazing at Rand Montgomery with a directness that he found vaguely unsettling. "We are kinsmen by marriage, but other than that, it is as if we had no bond whatsoever. Since you hold the title and estates of my daughter's heritage, I had hoped to come to know you. It would ease matters considerably when you arrive in England to claim your inheritance."

"I see your point," Rand said, "and I appreciate your thoughtfulness. And speaking of customs, the soirée that I have arranged for you is to be held tomorrow evening at a friend's home, Miss Copley. She has most generously offered the use of her home since mine has become a bit . . . crowded. I do hope that is convenient?"

"Of course," Jessamy said promptly. Did the ninnyhammer think she had *other* plans, for heaven's sake? "I shall most enjoy meeting your friends, Mr. Montgomery . . ."

"Rand," he reminded, and she inclined her head in a graceful tilt.

"Rand," she echoed. "It shall take some time to become accustomed to the more familar terms Americans prefer. It seems a bit awkward to me now."

"You shall have an excellent opportunity to practice at Miss Copley's tomorrow evening," Rand promised, pushing back his chair.

"You're not leaving already!" Jessamy exclaimed before she could catch herself. "Why, you've not had a bite to eat yet."

"I ate earlier," he replied in an amused tone. "And as I seem to recall your appreciation of our foods, *bon appétit*, my lady."

"Thank you," Jessamy said shortly, though her appetite

was gradually fading. Sparing Rand Montgomery a brief, vacant smile, she turned her attention to the foods William was offering her, deliberately ignoring the earl though she was actually very much aware of him.

Matters would be so much less complicated if he would only cooperate, and drat the fiend, he *would* be so handsome in his pale blue riding coat and those snugly fitting tan breeches. Gleaming boots that were as polished as a mirror clung to his calves, almost reaching his knees, and the white ascot he wore around his neck only set off his deep tan, making him appear both gentleman and rugged outdoorsman at the same time.

When her eyes lifted to his face, Jessamy found the earl regarding her with a mocking smile, and her fingers tightened reflexively around her silver fork. Had he seen the glimmer of admiration in her eyes? She sincerely hoped not.

"Do I have egg on my face?" she asked in a cold voice when he continued to gaze at her, and he shook his head.

"Not yet, Lady Jessamy, not yet..."

Jessamy stared after him as the earl departed, a tall, swaggering colonial who behaved as if he could handle any challenge—including an invasion by British petticoats. Well, she had not spent five years playing chess with the old earl and learned nothing! There were many gambits in the game of chess, and just as many in the game of life.

Selma Copley's townhouse was ablaze with light when the earl's carriage drew up in front. There seemed to be a thousand candles flickering in the darkness of the cool spring night, spraying pools of light across lawn and veranda as well as in the house.

William pulled down the steps and helped Jessamy descend from the well-sprung landau to the tiled walkway leading from the curved drive to the front steps. Faint strains of music drifted from the open door as she pulled her spangled shawl more tightly around her bare shoulders.

Pausing on the doorstep, Jessamy took comfort from the fact that the earl was beside her, for she did not know a single soul present. A milling throng of people chattered gaily, and from what she'd been told, she knew that among the guests were some of Baltimore's leading citizens, all come to meet and judge a British aristocrat.

Jessamy took a deep breath as the earl touched her elbow to guide her toward their hostess. Detaching herself from the crowd, the woman striding toward them with both arms outstretched to take Rand's hands was quite striking. She was dressed in a gown of ice-blue taffeta, with a low-scooped neck that showed off her ample charms to great advantage. Auburn curls gleamed under the glare of the lights, and her cheeks were flushed in a most becoming glow.

"Rand Montgomery!" the vision exclaimed. "How wonderful to see you again!"

"It's only been a few days," Rand remarked with a laugh, taking her outstretched hands in his.

"How's my pig?" Selma Copley asked with a flash of enchanting dimples. "Fatter?"

"Much fatter," Rand answered solemnly, and Jessamy suddenly recalled that on the day of her arrival, he had gone to purchase a hog. "May I introduce my guest?" Rand was saying, jerking her attention back to her hostess.

"Please! I've been dying to meet the guest of honor," Selma said, turning to Jessamy with a smile. "So you're Rand's cousin. He's told me a great deal about you, Lady Montgomery."

"Really? I'm flattered, Miss Copley. And may I say that you have a beautiful home . . ."

"Why, thank you. How long will you be staying in Baltimore, Lady Montgomery?"

"Oh, for an indefinite length of time. I simply wanted to meet my late husband's cousin, and perhaps acquaint him with some facts about his new acquisition . . ."

"Why, I heard about that! I think it's kind of exciting him being an earl and all; even if we don't have titles over here, I must admit that some of us are still impressed with all that . . ." Selma Copley's voice drifted away as she recognized new arrivals, and with a quick excuse to Rand and Jessamy, she was gone.

"Shall I escort you to the hors d'oeuvres table?" Rand murmured in Jessamy's ear. "I'm certain that you're hungry, as we did not eat dinner."

Slicing him a narrow glance, Jessamy found herself propelled in the direction of the long, linen-draped table covered with platters of pâté, wafer-thin slices of beef, ham, and chicken. There were plates of raw vegetables and fruit, and a variety of breads such as she had never seen before.

Rand held out a plate, then excused himself to speak to an acquaintance, a man he had not seen in some time.

"I'll be right back," he assured her, but Jessamy's attention was already on the buffet. She marveled at the ice carving dominating the table, and the seafood displayed on several silver platters. There was lobster, crab, shrimp, mackerel, cod, and trout, and she made a mental note to tell Nellie about the cunning way the chef had arranged the dishes.

"Are you certain you can eat all of that?" a low masculine voice murmured at her elbow, and Jessamy turned in surprise.

"I am certain of it," she stated firmly, smiling into a pair of handsome gray eyes. "Eating is my only vice."

"How Puritan," the gentleman observed with a smile. "I know who you are, Lady Montgomery, so do allow me to present myself to you. Jonathan Edwards, at your service." He made a small bow, fair hair falling over his brow as he did so. "Welcome to America."

"Thank you, Mr. Edwards."

"Do you intend to stay long . . . my lady?" A frown furrowed his forehead. "Is that the correct title? I find that I'm unaccustomed to meeting ladies and lords . . ."

"Lady is correct, yes," Jessamy answered. It was impolite to eat when one was talking, so she shifted her plate from one hand to the other, and cast a glance around the room for Rand. The earl was deep in conversation with the vivacious Selma Copley, smiling down at her in that way two people do when they have known one another for a long time. Just how well did he know Selma Copley, Jessamy wondered for a moment, then dismissed the thought. *How* long he'd known the lady didn't matter to her—she was only in America to secure Chastity's inheritance.

"Shall I hold your plate for you?" Jonathan Edwards was asking, reaching out to take it. "Buffets can be so unpleasant if one has not acquired the art of juggling plate, glass, and talking simultaneously, don't you think?"

"Yes, I do." Jessamy relinquished her plate with a smile. "Are you a native of Baltimore, Mr. Edwards?" she asked, determined to carry on a polite conversation.

"Oh no, I hail from New York. That's northeast," he added.

"How nice. I understand that New York City is a very large metropolis . . ."

The conversation continued in much the same light vein

for several minutes until the unfortunate Mr. Edwards made the gaffe of asking Jessamy's opinion on the recent conflict between England and America.

Stiffening, she fixed him with a cold gaze and said, "I do not care to discuss politics, Mr. Edwards. I find the recent unpleasantness most disconcerting, and as there were many casualties on both sides, it is a topic definitely unworthy of a soirée. Now, if you will excuse me..."

"I apologize," the young man said immediately, holding out a hand to detain her. "Do forgive me."

"My, my," an amused voice cut in. "Begging my cousin's pardon already, Edwards? You are quite impetuous, my lad!"

Flushing, the fair-haired young man started to explain to Rand but words failed him, so Jessamy offered, "I find that I am very sensitive about some subjects, and Mr. Edwards was not intentionally unkind. It is nothing."

Rand's amused glance drifted to Jessamy, noting her sparkling eyes and flushed face. "How fortunate for Mr. Edwards," he murmured. Their eyes met, and both could feel the sparks of tension between them.

Jonathan Edwards, for once at a loss for words, backed away from the pair with a muttered excuse, leaving Jessamy's plate of food on the buffet table.

"I believe you've been abandoned already, my lady," Rand drawled. "Did you hope to make a good impression at your first social gathering in Baltimore?"

"I still shall," Jessamy returned coolly. "One must establish certain guidelines in a conversation, and Mr. Edwards overstepped the boundaries of what I consider good taste, that is all."

"I agree," he surprised her by saying, and lifted a dark brow at her soft exclamation. "Did you think I would approve of the topic? It's not exactly *my* favorite object to discuss either, you know. Feelings still run pretty strong in America.''

"The same holds true in England." Leaning against the buffet table, Jessamy studied the tall, elegant gentleman before her, musing as to the complexities of Rand Montgomery. The presumed rough country bumpkin had turned into a suave, handsome gentleman, somewhat destroying her plans. Ah well, as in the game of chess, she would simply plan a new strategy. . .

Tucking her hand into the crook of his elbow, Jessamy smiled up at Rand with genuine interest.

"Why don't you tell me more about your customs in America?" she suggested. "I've noted that the carriages travel upon the right side of the road instead of the left. Is this customary?"

Smiling, Rand relaxed, and began to tell her about his country. He described some of the cities, told her about county fairs, and went on to talk about such diverse subjects as the advantages of the Louisiana Purchase in 1803. He spoke at great length, thoroughly fascinating Jessamy as she learned about the sprawling country she was visiting.

"Then you still have wild savages in your forests?" she asked at one point. "I had heard so, but dismissed it as idle gossip.''

"Oh yes, there are still native Indians here, but they are being pushed farther back from the cities with each passing day.''

"Is it true that there are still uncharted areas of wilderness in the West?" Jessamy asked.

Selma Copley had returned, bringing more of her guests to meet Rand's English cousin, and the discussion grew quite lively as all joined in, trying to tell Jessamy about America.

Stepping back two steps, Rand folded his arms across his chest and watched, admiring how Jessamy handled herself with poise and dignity. Once she looked up and found his eyes on her, catching that gleam of admiration, and she smiled inwardly. Perhaps Rand Montgomery would not be such a challenge after all . . .

✳ Chapter 5 ✳

"Oh, Mummy!" Chastity exclaimed, clapping her hands with delight. "You look so beautiful!"

Smiling, Jessamy turned her eyes from her adoring daughter to the mirrored reflection before her. "Do you think so?" she asked softly, though she agreed with her daughter. The cheval mirror *did* show a woman garbed in an extraordinarily lovely gown of blue shot silk. The gown had been ordered from Madame Pierre's before leaving London, with the intention of wearing it to the first ball she attended in America. It was styled in the latest fashion, with a low, square bodice, the short, puffed sleeves, and high waistline that was so popular. Shimmering folds of material fell from just under her breasts, caught by a wide band of satin riband, swirling gracefully around her ankles when she walked. Sara had arranged her hair in soft, loose curls, framing her oval face with pale wisps that were most becoming, and thin strips of matching blue silk had been wound among the shining curls.

Smoothing the elbow-length lace gloves she wore, Jessamy

examined the diamond and sapphire necklace circling her neck, a gift from Jamie on their first anniversary. Matching earrings dangled from her ears like captured stars from the sky, catching the light each time she moved her head, and a midnight-blue beaded bag swung from her wrist.

"You look like a princess, Mummy," Chastity said with a note of awe in her voice, and Jessamy turned to smile at her daughter, wondering suddenly if Rand would agree.

"Thank you, my precious. Of course, one cannot always judge a person by her clothes, but I *do* look rather regal for a mere commoner..."

"Pooh!" Margaret said, bustling into the room. "A commoner, indeed, Lady Jessamy! Why, you may not have the peerless lineage of some, but you are not exactly a peasant either!"

Laughing, Jessamy shrugged. "My only concern now is Chastity, Margaret. It's her future that matters." Her loving gaze rested on her sleepy-eyed daughter, who was knuckling her eyes with two chubby fists. "Off to bed, sweet," she murmured. "Margaret will take you."

With barely a whimper of protest, Chastity was lifted from the high four-poster bed into her nurse's arms, given a goodnight kiss, and carried from the room.

Giving herself a last-minute inspection, Jessamy was satisfied with the impression she would make on Rand's friends, Colonel Blackwell and his lovely wife, Corinne. Though she had met them only once, they seemed like a perfectly nice couple, who would have been welcomed in the homes of any of the *ton*. Corinne Blackwell was from England herself and still had two sisters living in London. She had been delighted to hear all the latest gossip concerning the fashionable Assembly rooms in King Street, Almack's, where Jessamy often had been coaxed into attending dances that she had found deadly dull. Now, to Corinne Blackwell, those dances seemed like elegant entertainment.

Pangs of homesickness had struck when Jessamy had regaled Corinne with tales of fashion, politics, and the latest peccadilloes committed by Prinny, the Prince Regent. She had even thought more sympathetically about the prince's garish dress and penchant for high living.

Ah well, this evening would be a huge success, even if Rand Montgomery should choose to behave like a complete widgeon.

Jessamy discovered that the new earl did indeed think she was lovely in her Paris gown of shot silk. His gaze returned to her again and again on the long carriage ride to the Blackwell home just outside the growing city limits of Baltimore. Hiding a satisfied smile behind a gloved hand, Jessamy busied herself with studying the passing scenery. There had been a definite spark of interest in his eyes, and that certainly furthered her plans. As of yet, there had not been what she considered a proper time to bring up Chastity's rightful inheritance. If she could, at the very least, charm the earl into naming her daughter as his legal heir, she would consider the journey a success.

Slanting a glance at his bemused countenance, she was still smiling when the carriage rolled to a halt in front of the well-lit portico of the Blackwell mansion.

Jessamy was pleased to find her hostess attired in the latest Continental fashion, which she laughingly confided to Jessamy had been absolutely *stolen* from under the nose of an acquaintance.

Corinne made a half-turn, skirts swirling gracefully. "I talked the dressmaker into letting me have it at a more profitable price than poor Vanessa Hargreaves," Corinne said. "As Vanessa had been more than a fortnight late in picking up the gown, the shopkeeper was quite willing to oblige . . ."

"It certainly is lovely," Jessamy said truthfully. Though the gown of light green silk with pink trim, all nicely layered with three tiers of Russian lace, was very pretty, it was not the style Jessamy could have worn. Only a petite, dark beauty such as Corinne Blackwell could be shown to advantage in that particular shade of green.

"Here come the wolves," Corinne whispered into Jessamy's ear, indicating several approaching gentlemen with a nod of her head. "Rand had best watch his manners, or one of these swells will snap you right out from under his nose!"

"I hardly think the earl worries on that account, Corinne," Jessamy said dryly, glancing at Rand. He stood a few short paces away, conversing most politely with a very distinguished-looking gentleman of advanced years, nodding occasionally to show his interest in their conversational topic. The new earl was a disturbingly handsome man, a fact many of the women present had also noted. *That* was apparent in the way they simpered when he glanced at them, or else ignored him most pointedly so that he would become intrigued at their obvious lack of interest.

"Oh," Corinne was confiding, drawing Jessamy's attention back to her, "I would think that Rand Montgomery is most definitely concerned about you, Lady Jessamy! Why, my husband—who is normally the very *soul* of discretion you understand—confided in me that Montgomery was making discreet inquiries as to the nature of the gentlemen who would be attending my ball this evening! And it had to do with *you*, my dear Lady Jessamy!"

"Really," Jessamy murmured thoughtfully, gazing at Rand with new eyes. Did the earl aspire to a match between them? But that was preposterous!

"Flummery," Jessamy said then, "pure flummery! Mr. Montgomery has never so much as hinted at an alliance between us, and I am certain he never shall. Not that it would matter a button to me either way, you understand, for I am comfortable with my situation as it is. I have been a widow for almost four years, you know."

"That is such a long time, and you are still quite young," Corinne Blackwell pointed out, delighted with the notion of assisting in matchmaking. She'd always fancied she had somewhat of a flair for that sort of thing, and now the idea of Rand Montgomery and his English cousin's widow making a suitable match piqued her interest. "Rand has such a lonely life, you know, all alone as he is, and he is quite dashing, don't you think?"

"Poppycock!" Jessamy was amused enough to exclaim with a laugh. "Oh, I don't mean about the earl's dash," she hastened to explain, "but I hardly think my cousin is what one would term 'lonely.' Somehow, it seems rather strange to label him with that epithet."

"Nonetheless," Corinne said firmly, loathe to relinquish her new idea, "I think you should be more sympathetic to Rand's plight. No family left, all his brothers killed in the recent . . . unpleasantness . . . and he is alone in the world."

"Well, now he has my daughter and myself to console him," Jessamy soothed. "We are his newfound family."

"Yes, I hear Rand is quite taken with your little girl. He was telling my husband that she is a cunning little thing, and quite bright."

"I like to think so," Jessamy answered, and the conversation—thankfully—veered to Corinne's own children, a boy and a girl who were, according to their beleaguered mother, holy terrors in the nursery. Jessamy hoped her surprise at the disclosure of Rand's opinion concerning Chastity had not shown itself to Corinne, for the reluctant earl had not shown such an interest in his niece to the child's mother! Indeed, she had quite given up hope of his ever becoming truly acquainted with Chastity. Jessamy made a mental note to question her daughter more thoroughly on the matter as soon as possible.

In the course of the evening, Jessamy and Rand were together very little of the time, usually just glimpsing one another across the crowded room. Jessamy found herself besieged with interest from the gentlemen, a flattering but quite exhausting ordeal that she found faintly puzzling. Certainly, she had never supposed herself to be homely, nor a cabbage-head, yet the unusual *vigor* with which some of the gentlemen made her acquaintance left her with the faint impression that there must be a dearth of suitable females of marriageable age and nature in America.

A particularly energetic gentleman by the name of Mr. Beauregard Cotter, who wore a spanking new waistcoat of the latest French design with rosebuds, was regaling her with tales of his exploits when she happened to catch Rand's gaze resting on her from across the room. His gaze was one that smacked of—it could only have been a mixture of amusement and satisfaction. How odd.

And a short time later, to Jessamy's bafflement, Rand paused by her side to murmur in passing, ''Avoid Cotter, my dear. He hasn't a feather to fly with . . .''

''Pardon?'' she began, but the earl had moved on, a young lady in blinding white satin clinging possessively to his arm with a very feline smile curving her mouth. Jessamy stared after him in bewilderment. It must be the press of the crowd that was making her so light-headed, and the air in Baltimore *was* much more humid than the cooler English climate, but why wasn't the earl making any sense? Why should it possibly matter to her if Cotter possessed any money... why, that fiend! Anger brought a most becoming flush to Jessamy's cheeks as she glared after the tall earl with a grimace of disgust. Did he really think her so lacking in the bone-box that she would actually set her cap for one of these American men?

The angry flush staining Jessamy's cheeks made her blue eyes seem even bluer, and added such a sparkle to the translucent depths that several admiring gentlemen remarked upon her flawless English complexion.

"Must be the constant rain over there," one young man said cheerfully. "I understand it does wonders for the skin."

"You may be quite correct," Jessamy answered politely, but her mind was considering and rejecting several possible scathing remarks to fling into Rand Montgomery's handsome face at the first opportunity. What a simple gudgeon he was if he thought that she was a scheming widow on the fly for a husband!

By the time the smoothly smiling earl made his way back to Jessamy, she was fuming with frustrated irritation. Her oval face, however, exhibited none of her inner turmoil as she smiled up at him and accepted his invitation to dance.

"Do you actually still have room left on your dance card?" Rand asked with a smile. "I would have thought you were turning men away by the droves, from all indications."

"Really? What a quaint notion," Jessamy replied, putting her hand in his and gliding onto the dance floor.

"Was that Henry Gibson I saw you dancing with earlier?" Rand queried with a lifted brow. "His family has been in politics since the Revolution . . ."

"Which revolution?" Jessamy interrupted innocently, then, "Oh, you mean the colonial *rebellion* of '76?"

Rand's eyes narrowed. "Yes, I suppose that one could refer to it as a rather large-scale rebellion. It was during that *rebellion* that my father was wounded. He lingered for years, but it eventually cost him his life, you know."

Slightly ashamed, Jessamy nodded and acknowledged, "Yes, the old earl had mentioned that to me."

"I'm sure he did. As for Henry Gibson, his family is quite well known, and he has an excellent reputation as a fine man."

Jessamy smiled, tilting back her head to gaze up at Rand with widely innocent eyes. "I have met so many nice people since arriving in America," she said.

"And do you intend to break all their hearts?" Rand asked lightly. "They seem to be falling at your feet . . ."

"Yes, it's so hard on my new slippers, having to step over all these men, but I'll manage," Jessamy returned with a sugary smile.

"You've adapted quickly," Rand observed. "Southern women are notorious flirts, and you seem to be an avid learner."

"Should I bat my lashes and simper?"

"Only if you feel like it, Lady Jessamy."

"Flirts are not indigenous to America, you know . . ."

"Ah, I'm well aware of that," was Rand's amused reply. "Even London ladies seem liable to the affliction."

"Are we in the same conversation?" Jessamy wanted to know, feeling a resurgence of anger. "I had thought we were discussing American men, not London ladies."

"Perhaps we should just dance and not talk at all," the earl rejoined smoothly, swinging Jessamy into the graceful steps of a waltz. For a moment they swung about the dance floor without speaking, Jessamy's skirts swirling in a bright curl of silk. What was he in a tear about? she wondered. He seemed . . . distracted. He held her stiffly, almost at arm's length, and when she flicked a glance to his face, she saw that his jaw was clenched, causing the faint scar to stand out more prominently.

Curiosity pricked her once again as she wondered how he had come by that wicked scar. Jessamy considered how it did not detract from his looks at all, but only made him seem more appealing somehow, like a rake. Of course, he probably *was* a rake, but that shouldn't matter to her at all once she had achieved her objective.

"Thank you for the dance," Rand murmured when the waltz ended, depositing Jessamy near the door to the small game room. "Shall I fetch you some punch?"

"Yes, please," she said primly, smoothing her skirts with one hand. "I should like that very much." Leaning against the archway, Jessamy watched as he moved across the crowded ballroom to the long buffet table holding brimming bowls of punch, admiring his graceful carriage. Perhaps she was being too sensitive and should not view the new earl with so much suspicion. After all, he had made every effort to present her to his friends, and had been nothing but correct in his manner to her. Yes, she should certainly be less judgmental of Rand Montgomery. . .

A burst of laughter caught Jessamy's atttention, and she turned to look into the game room, where there were several small tables set up for guests to play at cards. Immaculately clad servants hovered among the tables with silver trays bearing glasses of chilled wine, champagne, and punch. Smiling, Jessamy moved forward a few paces to watch.

Four women were playing a fast and furious game of whist, oblivious to all around them.

"That's above the sixth trick—I get one point," one woman announced cheerfully, then turned to continue her conversation with another player, ". . . and did you hear that he has made an offer of a substantial dowry to any man who wins her hand?"

"No! Really? I'm shocked that he even thought it necessary. . ."

"Well, there are extenuating circumstances according to my source," was the reply. "I understand he is trying to find her a husband quicky. He doesn't want the responsibility of a wife yet, *especially* one who is not an American citizen . . ."

"But she is so charming, I hear!"

"Have you met her?" another woman asked, slapping a card onto the table and declaring trump.

"Oh no, but I understand she is here tonight . . ."

"Is she? What does she look like?"

Jessamy, cheeks burning, began to suspect that *she* was the subject under discussion, that suspicion being confirmed when one of the women added in an airy tone, "I saw her arrive earlier with her cousin . . ."

Swallowing her mortification at being gossiped about like a common serving wench, Jessamy straightened her spine and gathered her self-righteous determination. So, Rand Montgomery intended to marry her off, did he? Well, he would soon discover how mistaken he could be! And just how big a dowry did he consider substantial, she wondered angrily. Ohhh! To think that he was offering a part of her daughter's rightful inheritance to anyone who would wed her and take her off his hands, just like . . . like an unwanted puppy! Well, it had oft been said that one who eavesdrops never hears good about themselves, but this was almost too much to bear.

Rand Montgomery chose that unfortunate moment to return with two crystal cups of punch, one of which he smilingly offered to Jessamy. Her fingers automatically curled around the fragile stem of the cup, clutching it as tightly as a weapon as she strove for self-control. Surely there was a way to beat this arrogant, egotistical colonial at his own game!

"Having a nice evening?" the earl asked idly, sipping at his punch.

"Yes, I certainly was," came the sharp answer.

"It's warm for so early in the year," Rand said after a few moments. His punch was half gone, and he slid Jessamy a narrow glance as if wondering why she was so stiff and silent. "Still angry with me for accusing you of being a flirt?" he asked lightly.

"Oh no, I'm not angry with you for *that*!" she said.

Montgomery's sharp ears caught her emphasis, and he asked carefully, "But you are angry with me?"

"Now, why would a lady be angry with a gentleman who has maligned her character and presented her to strangers as a pitiful, unwanted female?"

"I beg your pardon . . . ?"

"And well you should, you unpardonable fiend! You mutton-headed, odious cad! You should not only beg my pardon, you should cast yourself into the sea in contrition! You should suffer various and vile diseases! You should—"

"May I ask what dastardly deed I have committed to earn such hideous fates?" the earl interrupted coolly, fixing Jessamy with a thoughtful stare.

"I would not think you had to ask, my lord! Could this mean that you have committed more heinous deeds that I will not discover until I happen to overhear them? I hardly think—"

"You are working yourself into a state," Rand soothed, removing the crystal cup—which was in imminent danger of being crushed—from between her angry fingers. He set it down on the tray of a passing footman, and returned his attention to the furious lady before him. "Now what is this all about?" he asked calmly.

Beside herself, Jessamy snapped, "Just how large a dowry do you have to settle on me to be rid of your British burden, my dear Lord Wemyess?"

"Oh. That." The earl's tone was flat and resigned. "I never thought you would become so upset about such a trifling matter—"

"Trifling matter?" Jessamy gasped in outrage. "Didn't it ever occur to you to *ask* before you sought a husband for me? I do not intend to wed, my lord!"

"How unfortunate. It would be quite beneficial to you and your child. Think of the advantages—"

Jessamy lost control to the point where she stamped her foot in a futile gesture, eyes blazing as her chin lifted defiantly. "Advantages for whom—me or you? Oh, don't try and gull me, my dear Lord Wemyess, I fully realize that if I were to wed, you would be released of all responsibility for mine and Chastity's upkeep! Well, it won't work! You don't care a fig for Kenilworth, so it should go to my daughter—Jamie's daughter—by right. And even if I should marry, that won't change—"

"Let us discuss this in less crowded company," Rand said firmly, realizing that their heated discussion was beginning to draw attention. He forced a smile and said through clenched teeth, "Shall I call for the carriage?"

Jessamy's smile was a perfect copy of his as she answered demurely, "By all means, my lord. Do call for the carriage..."

✳ Chapter 6 ✳

By means of skillful conversation and adept avoidance, Rand was able to hold Jessamy's anger at bay for a time. Throughout the ride home from the ball he rode on top of the carriage with the driver, thus managing to sidestep any conflict on the way to his house; once home, he murmured a vague excuse about indigestion and fled from the entrance hall, leaving Jessamy seething in solitude, with only Wills as witness. She had stormed up the stairs, pausing on the landing to announce loudly that she would be most agreeable to the extermination of all American earls at the earliest possible moment, then slammed into her bedroom as noisily as she could.

Three days passed before she was finally able to confront Rand Montgomery with his deceitful, odious deed. She came close once, but the confrontation was barely avoided by the alert Wills, who warned his master of Jessamy's approach. The earl had actually fled his breakfast room, scurrying outside to vault into the saddle of the horse being held by his patiently waiting groom. Jessamy, arms akimbo, had halted on the front steps as Rand flew past her with a wide smile and a curt nod of his head.

"By Jupiter," she muttered in frustration, "he shall *have* to talk to me soon!"

"Soon" happened sooner than she'd hoped. In fact, it came the very next day, at the small dinner party she had planned for Corinne Blackwell. It gave Jessamy a certain amount of satisfaction to know that the earl had to attend the party or be publicly labeled a rude boor. Jessamy was enjoying herself immensely.

Dressed in a figured French muslin with a half-train, Jessamy looked quite becoming as she greeted her guests in the entrance hall.

"How do you do, Mistress Blackwell," she said to Corinne in her most formal manner, laughing when that lady pooh-poohed her greeting.

"Pooh! I daresay we are better friends than that, Jessamy! Don't give yourself airs because you are now a hostess!" In truth, the two ladies had shopped together only the day before, Corinne going into raptures over what she termed Jessamy's "slap-up taste in clothes."

Visiting the Baltimore shop of Mistress Dorothea, the two had discussed with the owner silks, satins, cambric, muslin, and crepes, and had closely studied the fashion plates sketched in *Ladies' Monthly Museum*, a London periodical. Corinne had chosen a ballgown of orange-blossom sarcenet for an upcoming ball, and had also ordered a fine jaconet muslin to be worn to smaller assemblies. Jessamy had favored only a Norwich shawl, to be worn carelessly around her elbows to add cachet to any common gown. They had admired Berlin silks trimmed with silk floss, velvet mantles, and waterloo hats, as well as ornamented bonnets for the lovely summer days ahead. All in all, it had been a most rewarding day out for both ladies.

When they returned from their shopping trip, both Jessamy and Corinne barely had time to freshen up before meeting the guests whom Jessamy had invited for a small dinner. Rand, looking quite handsome in a dark waistcoat, gray trousers, and a superbly tied cravat greeted the ladies at the bottom of the stairs with a polite, "It's wonderful, to see you again, Mrs. Blackwell." There was only a smile for Jessamy.

Colonel Blackwell, a handsome man in his mid-thirties, smiled pleasantly at the company. The colonel was one of those men much happier on a horse or in his fields than in a drawing room, but he loved his wife and did much to oblige her.

The other two couples Jessamy had invited arrived then, and the assembled group moved toward the drawing room for before-dinner drinks and stimulating conversation.

Dinner was a complete success. The service was good and the food excellent, and Jessamy gave a sigh of relief. One never knew how an affair would turn out, but it was especially difficult in a strange land with strange servants and a different menu.

When the dishes had been cleared away, she gave Wills a signal, and two of her English servants entered bearing a huge tray with a brandy-soaked strawberry trifle for dessert. The tray was set upon a cart and placed near the earl. While everyone exchanged curious glances, one of the maids snuffed the candles on the table. Only the chandelier overhead glowed with soft flickers of light, and a gentle breeze that wafted through the open window made the crystals vibrate with a tinkling sound like music.

Standing, Jessamy took a long taper from Drucilla and

moved to the cart, where she barely touched the dessert. It immediately flared into shimmering blue flames amidst a chorus of "oohs" and "ahhs" from the guests. Even the earl allowed himself a murmur of praise, and when his eyes met hers, Jessamy recognized a glimmer of appreciation in their depths.

After-dinner drinks consisted of claret for the ladies and brandy for the gentlemen, taken in the music room as the small study was designated.

"Do we play the pianoforte or cards?" Corinne asked lightly, gazing at the elegant spinet, and everyone laughed.

"Which do you prefer?" Jessamy returned. "I can arrange a game of cards, but unfortunately, I play only chess. I never had an opportunity to learn to play at cards."

"Really?" Lucretia Dinsmore said curiously. "I would have thought *everyone* in England played cards..."

"Oh, many do, but I tended the old earl for several years, and as he was housebound, we played chess quite a bit." She smiled. "He was too old and stubborn to play cards when he preferred chess, so my skill at cards is sadly lacking."

"How about your skill at chess?" Corinne teased, and Jessamy laughed.

"Not as good as it should be, I'm afraid. I never beat the earl at a single game..."

"It sounds deadly dull," Rand remarked with a quirk of one brow. "Perhaps you should have played for something other than pleasure."

"Oh? What do you mean?" she asked Rand.

Shrugging, he said, "It would have made the game more interesting, and perhaps you would have been a better player, if you had made a bet on the outcome."

"The earl had White's and Boodle's for that, I'm afraid,"

Jessamy answered stiffly. "He could always arrange for a bet to be made in one of those establishments if he so desired."

"And you? Did you really sit in the house day after day and play nothing but chess?" Lucretia asked. "I mean, did you *never* go out?"

"Oh, of course I went out, but as the earl was an invalid and had only a few visitors, I did spend much of my time with him."

Corinne gave a long sigh. "You are so self-sacrificing, Jessamy. I don't know if I would do the same . . ."

"Of course you would. He was family," Jessamy said. "I cared for him because I wanted to do so. Now, shall we hear a tune on the pianoforte, Olivia?" she said to the fragile wife of a Baltimore banker. "I understand you play . . ."

Olivia Wagner had barely finished playing a lively piece by Liszt when it was suggested that Rand bring out the cards. "Or a chess board for Jessamy," Corinne added with a teasing smile.

"Oh no," Jessamy laughed, "I will only play chess for high stakes now! Rand has shown me the error of my ways, and I will no longer squander my time in useless pursuit of unprofitable pleasure."

"Is that so?" Rand murmured, and Jessamy turned toward him. "What type of stakes did you have in mind, my lady?"

"Yes, that is so," she answered, and was almost trembling with the idea that had suddenly occurred to her. It was so simple, really, and a wonderful means of showing Rand Montgomery that he could not come the high-born swell with her when he was only a colonial. It would do him good to learn a lesson, and this would be such a perfect way of teaching him that he could not always predict a lady's behavior.

So she lifted her chin and smiled sweetly. "I have high stakes in mind, Mr. Montgomery. Dare you agree?"

He smiled modestly. "I'm a pretty fair hand at chess, but I find the game quite boring. I would not care to play you at it . . ."

"Oh, I wasn't thinking of playing *you*. I had in mind our earlier discussion . . ." She stepped close, gazing up into his eyes with a challenging stare. "You desire to see me wed, is that not true? So much so, in fact, that you have settled quite a generous dowry upon me."

Staring down at Jessamy, Rand was well aware of the fact that she had cornered him among his friends. Clearing his throat, he said shortly, "That is a well-known fact."

"Then, I propose to oblige you." Rounding on the assembled company, Jessamy stated firmly, "I will marry the first gentleman who can best me in a game of chess . . ."

✳ Chapter 7 ✳

June drifted past in a fragrant blend of bright flowers, summer breezes, hot days, and chess games. Jessamy found herself besieged with offers to play chess. Not one man had come close to beating her during that month. It was a point of contention between Jessamy and Rand.

Lying on a chaise longue in the garden, Jessamy mulled over the past weeks while sipping at a tall glass of lemonade. She had begun to cultivate quite a taste for the beverage, a fact that pleased Wills to no small extent.

"Mo' lemonade, ma'am?" he asked, hovering over her with a full pitcher, but she shook her head.

"No, not now, Wills, thank you. Have you been practicing your game?"

Grinning, Wills nodded his close-cropped head. "Yes ma'am, I sure have! I'm gittin' closer to that beaver ev'ry day!"

Jessamy laughed, a delightful sound that trilled as softly as notes from a harp. "And you shall have your new beaver top hat on the day that you learn the opening gambit, Wills, I promise.''

Pleased, Wills bobbed his dark head again, white teeth flashing in the sunlight. ''I'm close, ma'am, close!'' He paused, then added, ''And I ain't even told Master Rand about my learnin'. I'm not shore he'd like it.''

''Master Rand would not mind, I am certain,'' Jessamy answered, though she wondered if he would. Rand had not mentioned her chess games in almost a week, but she knew he was well aware of the defeat of all who had attempted to win not only a game of chess, but the hand of the lovely Lady Jessamy Montgomery. Her challenge had become the talk of Baltimore, the newest fashion. It was spoken of in all the drawing rooms and at all the teas. Everywhere she went she was accosted by determined gentlemen. It seemed that Americans loved a challenge.

The fresh breezes began to die in the heat of noon, and Jessamy finally rose from the chaise longue with a regretful sigh. It had been so peaceful resting in the garden, and heaven knows she had been bereft of peace lately. Thin muslin skirts dragged across the bright green blades of grass as she sauntered across the neatly clipped lawn to the house, thinking of her daughter. Chastity had been absorbed in a vast assortment of dolls when she had last seen her, some of which she did not recognize at all.

A faint frown puckered her brow as Jessamy swept into the long, cool hallway. The house smelled of lemon and beeswax, and the wood trim and tables gleamed in the light from the tall windows as she moved toward the downstairs parlor. Chastity's high, sweet laugh drifted from the parlor into the hall, and Jessamy was smiling when she pushed wide the doors.

Blinking, she stood in stunned surprise at the sight of

Rand Montgomery sitting cross-legged on the carpet, playing with Chastity. Clad in fawn trousers and a white lawn shirt open at the neck, Rand sat so that his long legs in their gleaming knee-high Hessians supported a bevy of porcelain dolls. He looked up, startled, and grinned sheepishly when he saw Jessamy in the doorway.

"Hullo," he said, "we've got company, Miss Chastity."

"Do sit still, Uncle Rand, or you will spill Persephone onto the floor," the child scolded, then flung over her shoulder, "Hullo, Mummy! Do you wish to play also? We're about to have our tea..."

"No," Jessamy began with a squeak, then cleared her throat and continued, "I...I...have other things to do. How...long...have you been playing in here, Chastity?"

"Only a little while, Mummy. Uncle Rand said I could, didn't you, Uncle Rand?"

"Yes, poppet, I did." Rand's dark eyes met Jessamy's for a moment, then slid back to the golden-haired child at his knee. "There's more room in the parlor than in her bedchamber," he said by way of explanation.

"I haven't seen this doll before," Jessamy said after a moment, stepping forward to lift an auburn-curled doll.

"Uncle Rand brought it to me. I named her Bonnie, and he said it was a nice name."

"Bonnie? After Bonnie MacLeod?" Jessamy asked. "I think that's lovely, Chastity."

Rand's brow furrowed thoughtfully. "Who is Bonnie MacLeod? The name sounds vaguely familiar..."

"It should—she is a second cousin on the Montgomery side of the family," Jessamy said dryly. "Of course, you've never been to England or Scotland, so you would not know that."

"No. I wouldn't." Rand's eyes rested upon Jessamy's

flushed face, and his lips quirked in a slightly mocking smile.

"I miss Bonnie sometimes," Chastity said in her clear, childish voice, "and I miss England and Kenilworth, too. You should come to Kenilworth, Uncle Rand. You would like it so . . ."

"I shall do that one day, Miss Chastity," Rand said, carefully laying her dolls on the small blanket she had spread upon the carpet. "But while you're in America, I will take you to my country home. It's very big—maybe not as big as Kenilworth—but quite pretty, with lots of trees and flowers, and even a few ponies . . ."

Clapping her hands with delight, Chastity exclaimed, "Ponies! Oh, I do so love to ride! I have my very own pony at home, don't I, Mummy! When shall we go, Uncle Rand?"

"Soon. Now I must talk with your mother, poppet. You stay here, and I will tell Margaret where to find you."

"Don't tell her too soon, or she will make me take a nap," Chastity begged, gazing up at Rand as he surged to his feet in a swift, lithe motion.

"I'll give you a few more minutes," he promised, taking Jessamy by the elbow and escorting her to the door.

"Well," she said when they were in the hallway, "I had the distinct impression you considered children a distasteful burden who should be ignored until after reaching their majority."

"That was until I met Chastity," Rand teased. "She's a delightful child."

"I certainly think so." Jessamy wandered across the hall and into the small study often used as a music room. Stepping to the pianoforte, she ran her fingers lightly over the polished ivory keys, listening to the crescendo of tinkling notes.

"Do you play?"

"The pianoforte—or chess?" Jessamy asked, turning to face him with an arched brow.

"I know you play chess well," he returned dryly. "That has been proven during the past few weeks."

Smiling, Jessamy leaned against the delicately carved pianoforte, regarding Rand with a steady gaze. "Does that distress you, my lord?"

"Why should it distress me that you have made marriage a game?" he mocked.

"But it was you who deemed it necessary to set me up as a matrimonial prize," Jessamy pointed out firmly. "I merely set my own guidelines. After all, I would not wish to wed a man who cannot even best me in a simple game of chess . . ."

"Rubbish!" Rand said rudely. "That is not the reason at all, and you know it. You were angry because I had not consulted you before making my very generous offer of a substantial dowry!"

"No, I am angry because you even considered making such an astounding offer!" Straightening, Jessamy took several steps forward, facing Rand with lifted chin and fiery eyes. "I think it simply a harebrained scheme concocted by a pudding-hearted fiend who does not wish to be bothered with female relatives . . ."

"Oh, you do!" Drawing himself up to his full—and quite impressive—height, Rand glared down at Jessamy. "Then what is your suggestion, my fine English lady? Do I just take up housekeeping with you and your daughter, or do I callously toss you from your home with no more ado? Either way, I am considered the cad . . ."

"And rightly enough, all things considered . . ."

"Do you actually think I would dispossess a mere child of her ancestral home without recompense?" Rand exploded. "No, don't answer that. I see your answer in your eyes."

Reaching out, he grasped Jessamy firmly by her arm, half-dragging her to a corner of the room.

"What are you doing?" she gasped, wondering fearfully if he had lost all control of his reason.

"Sit down, madam, and play a *real* opponent in a game of chess," he ordered, swinging her to a chair placed by the small chess table.

"No! I refuse to dignify your ridiculous scheme any longer," she began, but was cut short by Rand's soft rejoinder.

"Not even if Kenilworth is the stake, my lady?"

Jessamy's rebellious knees refused to support her, and she immediately sank to the comfort and security of the chair.

"Kenilworth?" she echoed.

"Yes. All you have to do is win the game, and I will sign the papers making Kenilworth and all it entails legally yours," he said through clenched teeth.

"Fair enough, but what if I lose?"

He smiled. "I keep Kenilworth without any more fuss, to do with it as I wish."

Taking a deep breath, Jessamy nodded. "Agreed," she said. "White or black?"

"You choose."

Hesitating, Jessamy finally chose white. She needed to observe Rand's strategy, so she intended to draw him out slowly. The small mantel clock ticked loudly as the game commenced, with both players soon absorbed. Pawns, knights, and rooks fell by the wayside, but neither of them could force the other's king into a position in which it would be subject to capture, or checkmate. Once Jessamy had Rand in check, but he managed skillfully to avoid the final denouément with an expert strategy that left her aghast.

Sitting back, she gazed at the man opposite while he studied the board. She was quite confident that he could not force her into checkmate, yet there was a certain amount of doubt that made the game much more interesting. This Rand Montgomery was no goosecap, she thought. He played with efficient ease, and she felt a moment of gratitude to the old earl for being such a formidable player all those years. Leaning an elbow on the table, she rested her chin in her palm, watching as the earl maneuvered her into a check position. She tapped her fingers against her chin for several moments, considering, then executed a move that extricated her from check.

"I believe we can consider this a draw," Rand said after a few moments, and she agreed.

"Yes. Shall we declare no winner?"

Scraping back his chair, Rand leaned one arm over the curved back and nodded. "You're quite good," he remarked casually. "I had not thought you could hold out against me."

"Really?" Smiling, Jessamy rose and moved to the silver tray on the sideboard that held several decanters. "*I* had not thought you would get past the opening gambit, my lord."

"You *do* have a poor opinion of me, then!"

"Oh no, only a poor opinion of your strategies," she returned, pouring a half glass of claret.

A reluctant smile tugged at Rand's mouth. "You are quite a woman, Jessamy Montgomery," he said softly.

"I shall choose to take that as a compliment . . ."

"It is. I've never met a woman quite like you."

"I should think not." Jessamy took a sip of claret. "I should think that you never will, my lord."

"Don't call me that!" he flared. "My name is Rand."

"Ah yes. It's just that it's so easy to think of you as the new earl . . ."

"I'm an American," he said testily.

"So I noticed." Jessamy took another sip of claret, gazing at Rand over the rim of the goblet. "An American at Kenilworth would seem so strange," she mused, "yet I suppose I must recall that you are, after all, the rightful owner, while Chastity and I have been cast upon the whim of fate . . ."

"I would hardly call a townhouse in London, a country home in Devonshire, and holdings in Scotland being 'cast upon the whim of fate,'" the earl said sarcastically. "You were not exactly left penniless."

"Yet, Chastity's true home is Kenilworth. She has known no other. I simply want what is my daughter's by right."

"Damme, but you're a hardheaded, stubborn female! Will nothing else satisfy you?"

"Nothing."

"Why should I yield what was left to me by my uncle? He obviously wanted me to have it."

Fretful shadows leapt in Jessamy's eyes. Hadn't she asked herself that question a hundred times? Why had the old earl left Kenilworth to this American who didn't care a button for it?

"Cat got your tongue?" Rand taunted, moving to stand close to her. "Or do you prefer not to answer?"

But how could she speak when he was so close—when she could almost count the spiky lashes shading his eyes, and could feel the heat he generated? And why should she even notice how his shirt was open to bare his chest?

Jessamy's heart began to thud loudly, and she found it difficult to breathe with Rand standing so close.

Then Rand was reaching out to stroke her face with the backs of his fingers, a smile pressing against his mouth that wasn't taunting or mean, but full of promise.

"You're quite lovely," he murmured, "but I suppose you know that. It must turn your head to have every man in Baltimore county courting you."

Instinctively, Jessamy's hand rose to grasp his fingers. Startled by his action, her eyes flew to his, recognizing the warm light in the depths, and unaccountably her breath quickened.

"But then again," Rand was saying huskily, "you turn the head of every man in Baltimore county..."

He was going to kiss her, Jessamy knew then, and she didn't know whether to retreat or stay; but then the decision was taken from her as Rand leaned forward, his mouth touching her lips with light tenderness. Flushed with confusion, she closed her eyes and tilted back her head, floating on the riot of emotions coursing through her.

It was over as quicky as it had begun. Rand withdrew and stepped back, saying regretfully, "I should not have done that..."

Jessamy's eyes snapped open, and her cheeks deepened to crimson. "Never apologize for kissing a lady, sir," she advised tartly, jerking away. "It is exceedingly bad manners, and shows a lack of breeding!"

Gathering her dignity about her like a cloak, she pivoted and sailed from the music room without another word, more shaken than she would have liked to admit. How dare he kiss her and then apologize? And why had she enjoyed it so much...

✳ Chapter 8 ✳

The customary peace of early morning was disturbed the following day, when Jessamy was awakened by the unusual sounds of bumping furniture, thumping doors, and the chatter of servants. The gauzy netting draped around her bed was stirred by a breeze from the open window, ballooning when her door opened to admit Chastity.

"Mummy!" the child cried excitedly, parting the netting to clamber onto the high bed beside her mother. "Isn't it just grand? I can hardly wait to go, and Uncle Rand has promised I can choose my own pony . . . he says they run wild on an island not far from here. I think it's called Chin . . . Chin . . . Chincotease . . ."

"Chincoteague," Margaret corrected helpfully, coming up behind her small charge. "The ponies are descendants of survivors from the Shetland Islands that were shipwrecked years ago. They run wild, and are hard to catch and even more difficult to tame."

"How do you know so much?" Jessamy asked, rather overwhelmed by such vigorous activity so early in the morning. "And whatever is Chastity talking about? Going where?"

"Idlewood!" Chastity blurted before Margaret could answer. "We're going to Idlewood."

"Margaret . . ?" Jessamy's tone was plaintive.

"Come, Miss Chastity!" her nurse said in a severe tone that the child did not dare question. "Let me answer your mother's questions while you go wash your face." When Chastity had slid meekly from the bed, bare feet padding across the floor, Margaret turned back to Jessamy. "She's just so excited at the prospect of getting to the country," she said.

Taking a deep breath, Jessamy sat up in the bed. "When are we going to the country, may I ask?"

"You didn't know?"

"Know what! I'm getting the absolute fidgets just trying to decide what flummery you're talking . . ."

"Why, the earl has gone on ahead, but has left instructions for us to join him at his country home. I've had Sara and Drucilla packing since first light this morning."

"Why aren't we staying here?" Jessamy pushed at a strand of hair hanging in her eyes, cross and impatient. Why hadn't Rand said anything to her?

"The earl said he always closes up his townhouse in the summer, to go to the country."

"How quaint," Jessamy remarked sourly. "And I suppose we are to just pack up and join him?"

"I believe that is the idea, yes," Margaret replied.

"What a perfectly ghastly manner in which to be wakened," Jessamy sighed, flinging back the coverlet. "I feel as if I have misbehaved and am being sent off like a naughty child."

Catching Margaret's curious gaze, Jessamy wisely decided to be silent. It would do her no good to tell her old nurse how she had allowed Rand Montgomery to kiss her in the downstairs music room, no good at all. She had made a complete cake of herself, and now it seemed as if she was being packed off to the country for her sin.

The countryside in Maryland was a great deal different from the country in England, Jessamy discovered with trepidation. England possessed gentle, cultivated fields, rolling meadows, and shaded woods, but even the wilder heaths and moors did not seem quite so *dangerous* as the forests beyond Baltimore.

"Perhaps it's because it is a newer country," Margaret suggested. "After all, England has been civilized for quite some time, while America..."

"Has yet to be civilized," Jessamy cut in crankily. She shifted on the carriage seat, holding a sleeping Chastity in her lap. Why was it children could sleep quite peacefully anywhere, even on the bumpiest roads? "And it's almost unbearably hot," Jessamy muttered, pressing a drenched hanky to the perspiration beading her forehead and dampening tendrils of hair hanging limply over her ears. "I can hardly bear the heat."

"This journey may be the death of me," Margaret moaned a few moments later, fanning herself with the vellum-and-ivory fan she'd brought. "I don't see any signs of habitation out here, only trees and more trees!"

The carriage dipped into a rut, swayed, then righted as the perfectly matched bays pulled it along without a pause, leaving Jessamy and Margaret clutching the sides of the vehicle with white-knuckled fingers.

"Don't be a goosecap, Margaret," Jessamy said faintly. "You know Charles and the others are not far behind us."

"How comforting. Can you see Charles wrestling a bear, my lady?"

In spite of the heat and dust, Jessamy began to grin. "No," she said truthfully, "I cannot! What widgeons we are, even to agree to travel along this . . . this . . . cowpath!"

"Is there a bear, Mummy?" Chastity asked sleepily, rubbing at her eyes, and Jessamy soothed her with the assurance that there was no bear within miles.

"Go back to sleep, pet," she said softly, "and we will soon be there."

Settling back into her mother's lap, the child had soon fallen back into restless slumber, her weight heavy against Jessamy.

"Shall I hold her?" Margaret offered, but Jessamy shook her head.

"No, I'm already rumpled and sticky with heat. One of us might as well look presentable when we arrive."

Letting her head fall back against the dusty velvet cushions, Jessamy closed her eyes, willing the journey to end. Perhaps she should not be so precipitate as to cast herself headlong into a situation which she might find distasteful, she mused. After all, she had not seen the earl since their little confrontation in the music room; what if he looked down his nose at her?

Jessamy repressed a shudder of dismay. Somehow, the notion that Rand might find her lacking in some degree was highly distressing. Why should she care what her cousin thought of her? She had only come to America to coax him into naming Chastity his heir, hadn't she? She had no possible interest in the man at all, none whatsoever.

Then why, she wondered, did she see his handsome face whenever she closed her eyes? Cornflower blue eyes snapped open immediately. To her surprise, Jessamy realized that the carriage had halted. It was quite still and quiet outside, and she felt a tremor of nerves.

"What is it, Margaret?" she queried, but her old nurse was already sticking her head out the window of the landau to discover the reason for the delay.

"I say, driver, what is the meaning of this?"

The driver was the same man who had transported them from the dock upon their arrival in America.

"I'm picking up a passenger," Boris explained.

"A passenger?" Jessamy echoed. "Who? And where will he sit, pray tell?"

The inside of the carriage was crowded with boxes and portmanteaus that would not fit upon the roof of the landau without being crushed. It had been imperative that such items survive the journey, so they had been placed inside the carriage with Jessamy and Margaret.

"But . . . there's no room," Margaret protested. A faint cloud of dust began to settle upon the coach and its occupants, making Jessamy sneeze and Margaret cough. Chastity slept blithely on.

"Take Chastity," Jessamy instructed, shifting the sleeping child to Margaret. "I intend to find out the meaning of this delay!"

When the carriage door swung open, a man scrambled to put down the steps, and Jessamy descended from the landau. Small puffs of dust rose with every step as she made her way determinedly to the front of the carriage, shielding her eyes with one hand as she squinted up at the driver.

"Boris, I insist that you explain this delay more fully," she began, but he was nodding toward the road they had just traveled.

"Here they come," he announced, and Jessamy turned,

blinking against the bright sunlight and ever-present haze of dust.

The shadow of a horse and rider could barely be discerned, loping toward the halted vehicle amidst a cloud of dust. As he drew nearer, Jessamy could make out the tall, familiar shape of Rand Montgomery, but a much different Rand from the one she was accustomed to seeing.

This Rand was garbed in soft clothing sewn from the animal hides known as buckskin, and he wore quite unusual boots upon his feet. A wealth of fringe hung from the front of the jacket he wore and the seams of his long, snug-fitting trousers. The boots, which rose to his knees, were made of the same soft material as his jacket but with a much thicker fold forming the soles. Jessamy's astounded gaze noted odd details, such as the fact that the coat had no collars or lapels, nor even sleeves, and the wide belt he wore around his lean waist sprouted the hilt of a quite wicked-looking knife. Was that the butt of a pistol protruding from the belt? Her gaze flew to his face in alarm.

"Good afternoon, Boris," he was saying, edging his mount nearer the carriage. It was then that Jessamy saw Rand carried a passenger with him, a small, brown-skinned boy wearing much the same garments as Rand. "Thanks for waiting on Jimmy," Rand said as the boy swung down from the horse to land in the dust on his bare feet. "I was hoping I hadn't missed you."

"I waited, Mister Rand," Boris replied, puffing on his pipe. "Knew you'd be along directly."

Rand's gaze flicked to Jessamy. "I hope it won't impose on you too much to have Jimmy ride to the house with you," he said, in a tone that clearly indicated he didn't really care at all if it did. She glanced at the child, who regarded her with a stoic expression, his long dark hair hanging in twin braids on each side of his head. He was darkly beautiful, with that peculiar, exotic look about him.

Lifting her hands in a helpless gesture, Jessamy began, "There really isn't much room inside, but . . ."

"Why not?" he cut in rudely.

Well aware of the bedraggled picture she must make, Jessamy nonetheless strove to keep her voice cool and calm. "We were forced to put some of our things inside instead of on top where they might be crushed."

"I can take care of that," Rand said, swinging down from his horse. He strode swiftly to the carriage and began yanking out hatboxes and portmanteaus, handing them to Jessamy's servants, Charles and Richard, who had caught up with them. He worked so quickly and smoothly that he soon had the last box out, shoving it into Jessamy's arms when it seemed that the men's arms were already full. "That should take care of it," Rand said pleasantly. "I shall see you at the house, my lady. Be good, Jimmy," he added to the boy, who watched impassively, blue eyes lively and alert in his nut-brown face.

Staggering under the large hatbox she held, Jessamy was just able to utter a muffled "Wait!" as Rand reined his horse in a circle and nudged it into a canter. As he vanished in a cloud of dust, Jessamy's eyes turned to the curiously watching boy, who regarded her with his head tilted to one side. She cleared her throat of dust and said as nicely as she could, "Hello, Jimmy."

He said nothing, only gazing at her with wide clear eyes that seemed much too light for his dark skin. The boy's parentage was obviously part native Indian, Jessamy decided, wondering who he was and whom he belonged to.

"Well," Margaret said helplessly, a wide-awake Chastity in her lap, "bring the boy inside and let's be on our way."

"Oh yes, Mummy! I like him tremendously already," Chastity said, earning the boy's attention. His dark head shifted in her direction, and his eyes widened at the sight of the fair, fragile child with golden curls perched in the carriage.

He was inside the landau in one smooth motion that reminded Jessamy of a cat, leaping in through the open door to land on the balls of his feet, startling a squeal out of poor Margaret. "Good gracious!" the poor woman moaned, fanning herself again. "I don't know about this, I just don't know at all!"

✳ Chapter 9 ✳

As the shiny black landau rounded a bend in the road, the air unbelievably became cooler and sweeter. A profusion of wild vines grew along the roadside, with tiny yellow and white flowers among the oval leaves giving off a heavy fragrance that Jessamy couldn't quite place.

"Honeysuckle," Chastity said, adding at her mother's curious glance, "Uncle Rand showed me how to pull off the flowerets and suck the sweet honey from them."

"When?"

"Not long ago," the child answered, turning back to smile at the boy sitting quiet and solemn on the floor of the carriage. "Do you like to do that?"

He nodded, his eyes still fixed on the small golden creature before him as if she was made of spun sugar.

"Then we shall do that as soon as possible," Chastity announced grandly, turning back to gaze out the window.

The landau turned off the main road, winding along a curving drive through a leafy canopy of oak trees that blew gently with the wind. A riot of color met their eyes in a thick border along the drive—marigolds, peonies, petunias, geraniums, and other blossoms that were too many and varied for Jessamy to name. She stared in awe at the huge emerald sweep of lawn that stretched up to a sprawling house of brick and white-painted wood.

Margaret made a peculiar sound in the back of her throat, and the two women exchanged wide-eyed glances. "It . . . it's beautiful," Jessamy murmured, and Margaret nodded agreement.

As the carriage slowed, Jessamy glimpsed a formal garden behind the house, complete with marble statues in graceful Grecian poses. And did she hear the subtle tinkling of a fountain?

Idlewood lay like a beautiful lady before them, its slender, graceful columns stretching from the shallow brick porch that sat flush on the ground, all the way to the top of the second story. The eight masonry columns were sparkling white, but curiously painted with black stripes, Jessamy thought.

Boris drew the vehicle to a halt, and Charles scurried forward to bring down the carriage steps and open the door. Pausing, Jessamy looked up from where she was stepping to see a large, ebony-faced woman waiting on the front porch, her broad face seamed with a big smile. A bright red scarf completely covered her head, and she wore a gold hoop in each earlobe. She made a brief curtsy to Jessamy, then turned a scowling face to Boris.

"What done took you so long!" she hissed. "You done s'posed to be here an hour ago! I fixed up a fine dinner for these here ladies, and now it done got cold!"

"Excuse me," Jessamy said softly, "but there's no need to scold poor Boris. He only followed instructions."

"Hmmph! Boris, he always slow and late! You'll find out

soon enough. Now come on in the house, ladies. I knows you is plumb wore out from yore trip . . .''

Margaret and Chastity descended from the carriage, followed by the exotic boy. When he leaped to the porch, the boy was immediately collared by the large black woman.

"There you is! I done been lookin' for you, too, rascal! Here!—you Jimmy!'' she said with an affectionate shake of her pointed finger. "Git on up them stairs and git cleaned up before Mistah Rand gits home and sees you like this!''

Flinging her a faintly defiant look, the boy managed to shrug from her grasp and flee into the house, dusty heels flying high.

"That boy,'' the woman said to the group in general, "he done gonna be the death of me, he sure is. Now, I'm Pauline, Polly to most, and Mistah Rand, he asked me to see to your comfort.''

Jessamy's curiosity burned to discover exactly whom the child belonged to, but she could not ask without being too obvious. Was he a relative of Rand's? A servant? Why was he being treated as a member of the household instead of a servant, if that was the case? Her questions went unuttered and unanswered as she found herself herded into the house by Polly, with all the skill and tact of a field marshal. Polly bustled behind with Margaret and Chastity—whom the woman immediately decided was a perfect little golden angel. Margaret kept an anxious watch on her charge, slightly suspicious of the overbearing housekeeper's take-charge attitude. Chastity was *her* responsibility and no one else's!

Pausing in the large, airy entrance hall, Jessamy gazed about her with interest. This house had much more personality than Rand's townhouse; it seemed to reflect the man more closely. Wide double doors at the opposite end of the long hall had been left open to allow in cooling breezes from the garden, and the gentle scent of bright summer flowers filled the air.

"Why...it's so cool in the house," Jessamy observed with soft surprise.

Polly nodded vigorously. "Yes'm. Mistah Rand had this house built to be cool. He's real proud of this house, he is," she said, moving through the hall to fling wide the doors to a double parlor. "It cost him a lot to build this house, and then the war done come and it almost got burnt to th' ground! If'n it hadn't been for Mistah Rolfe and Mistah Rowan, why it woulda plumb been gone when them..."

Stumbling to a halt, Polly seemed to realize suddenly that she had almost said too much. Her pudgy hands twisted a fold of her white apron between her fingers as she glanced anxiously to see if Jessamy had taken offense. Jessamy's smile eased her fears, and Polly relaxed slightly.

"Mister Rolfe and Mister Rowan were Rand's older brothers, weren't they?" Jessamy said. "I seem to remember that they were killed in the conflict. My husband was lost during that time also."

"Yes'm. A powerful lot of peoples was killed, I reckon."

"War is always devastating, Polly. Is this a portrait of the family?" Jessamy stepped closer to the fireplace, gazing up at the gold-framed painting on the wall.

"Yes'm. That's Mistah Rand's momma and daddy, and the three boys when they was little. Lord, but they was powerful ornery when they was young'uns!"

Jessamy's mouth curved into a smile. "Yes, I suppose they would be," she murmured, studying the handsome family portrayed in a setting of sky and trees. There was even a family dog at the feet of one of the older boys, a tan-and-white spaniel with lolling tongue and bright eyes.

"Is that Mister Rand in his mother's arms?" she asked Polly, knowing that it must be. He was the youngest, only about two years of age, regarding the world with huge dark eyes and the same devastating smile. His hair had been lighter then, more like his father's, whereas now he resembled the darker coloring of his mother.

"Mistah Rand looks just like his daddy," Polly reminisced with a sigh. "Don't you think so, ma'am?"

"Yes, he certainly does resemble his father," Jessamy answered, turning away from the portrait. "I had heard that Colin Montgomery was a handsome man."

"He surely was," Polly agreed, then slanted a glance toward a slender black girl hovering in the doorway. "Your meal is ready, ma'am, whenever you want to eat."

It was half an hour before Jessamy entered the dining room. She had insisted upon washing off the dust from the road and had been pleasantly surprised by the first-floor convenience room. It eliminated the necessity of climbing the curved stairs to the second floor just to wash one's face or hands, often a tiring feat due to the bulky volume of one's skirts.

Another pleasant surprise awaited her in the dining room. The walls had been painted blue, with a rich cream trim almost the color of wheat, and gently swagged drapes of blue and cream hung over the multi-paned windows. Shelves flanked the fireplace, displaying Wedgewood plates and bowls and a huge soup tureen. Faux-bamboo chairs lined an oval eighteenth-century table set with three places. The centerpiece was a K'ang Hsi bowl filled with fragrant peonies floating near the brim. English flatware with agate handles nestled close to the Spode plates, and a cobalt and silver salt trencher waited near three brass candlesticks of the Federal period.

The entire room conveyed a sense of welcome and warmth which most formal dining rooms in English manors lacked.

"Will your daughter and maid be joining you, ma'am?" a young girl asked, doing her best to bob a quick curtsy.

Jessamy smiled. "No, they will be taking a tray in their room."

Polly swept into the dining room with a platter of food that emanated an unfamiliar but delicious odor. "I done had it sent up, Sukey," she said to the girl. "You can go on back to the kitchen now, and be sure that Jimmy cleans his plate . . . Do your little girl eat supper with you at night, ma'am," she directed to Jessamy in the same breath, "or should I set a place for her in the kitchen?"

"Oh no, she will eat in her room," Jessamy replied, seating herself in one of the chairs. "Will Mister Rand be joining us tonight for dinner?"

"You mean supper?"

"Yes . . . supper."

"I don't rightly know, ma'am," Polly said, placing the platter carefully on the table. "He's out in the fields lookin' after some of the workers."

"Isn't there an overseer to look after the slaves?"

"Slaves!" Polly expostulated. "Oh no, ma'am, we ain't got no slaves at Idlewood! Why, Mistah Rand done freed all his slaves a long time ago. We's all free," she added, lifting her double chins proudly.

"I see," Jessamy murmured thoughtfully. One more facet to Rand Montgomery's increasingly complex personality . . . a man who freed his slaves when slavery was so popular.

"Have some cracklin' bread, ma'am," Polly urged, pushing forward a platter of what looked to be fried bread. "We got hot buttermilk biscuits, too, and roast chicken, spinach salad, sweet pickles I made myself, and crowder peas, butter beans, and fried corn.''

Jessamy's head spun with the array of dishes Polly named as they were brought in by several uniformed servants, but before long she had sampled everything, including another bread—did all Americans eat so much bread? she wondered— Polly named as cornbread. There were dishes of stewed peaches, fresh strawberries and cream, and even a steaming blackberry cobbler.

''You sure do eat a lot for such a tiny thing!'' Polly said admiringly. ''I seen field hands that can't put away as much vittles as you can, ma'am.''

Patting her mouth with one corner of a cream-colored linen napkin, Jessamy smiled. Never in England would servants speak so familiarly and often. Here they were treated more as members of the family than as simply hired servants, yet she found it uniquely refreshing. It was quite a change from stilted formality.

''What does one do in the country, Polly?'' she asked, sipping water from a Waterford glass. ''I suppose there is not a great deal to do out here.''

''Oh no, ma'am! Why, Mistah Rand already has a picnic planned!''

''Ah yes, I'd forgotten about that. He purchased a hog for the occasion, if I recall correctly.''

''Yes'm, and there's going to be good eatin', I can tell you that! Miss Selma knows how to plan picnics, too.''

''Does she live near Idlewood?'' Jessamy asked curiously. ''I seem to recall Mr. Montgomery mentioning that she did.''

''Yes'm. Highland—where she lives—is only a short ride away.''

"Well," Jessamy said, rising from the table, "that certainly makes it convenient, doesn't it?"

"Yes'm. Mistah Wayne—Miss Selma's brother—he's kinda crippled up since the war, and he and Mistah Rand has always been good friends. Mistah Rand, he goes to visit Mistah Wayne as often as he can get away."

For a brief moment, Jessamy wondered if Wayne Copley was the only person Rand chose to visit at Highland, then dismissed the thought immediately. After all, it was none of her business whom Rand Montgomery chose to visit, and she really shouldn't care at all.

"Thar's a cool breeze out on the veranda," Polly was suggesting, "and a real comfortable chair if'n you want to relax a while, ma'am."

"That sounds like an excellent idea," Jessamy said. "I think I shall do that very thing, Polly, thank you."

It was pleasant on the wide veranda overlooking the garden, and Jessamy reflected that the garden was a delight to behold. A huge circular bed dominated the lawn, bordered by snowy clumps of sweet alyssum, with violets, eglantine, London pride, love-lies-bleeding, heart's ease, gillyflowers, polyanthus, sweet william, wallflowers, honesty, spicy pinks, foxgloves, flower-de-luce, Canterbury bells, and monkshood bursting with an explosion of color. A handmade hickory ladder leaned against an outbuilding, decorated with sprays of wild roses that twined around the warped rungs, adding a piquant touch to the garden.

Leaning back against the pillows of a wicker rocker, Jessamy slowly fanned herself with an Italian fan of parchment leaf decorated with a pen-and-ink drawing depicting the "Feast of Belshazzar." Trills of birdsong hung sweetly in the air, drifting on the soft breeze that lifted straying tendrils of Jessamy's pale hair in playful wisps. The warmth of the summer sun, the heavy scent of magnolia blossoms, and the buzz of bees combined to cause her eyelids to grow heavier and heavier.

Just as her head bobbed in a most disgraceful manner, Jessamy heard the faint thud of horse's hooves and sat upright, unwilling to be caught napping like an old woman. Looking around, she didn't see anyone for a moment, then slowly became aware of a partially hidden path leading past the veranda and down to the stables.

"Hullo," a deep voice said, jerking her head around. "I almost caught you napping, didn't I?" Smiling, Rand regarded her with a quirked brow as he led his horse near the veranda railing. Sunlight made the sorrel's hide gleam as brightly as copper, and the fine breeding of the animal was apparent in the clean lines and well-molded head, a fact Jessamy would have appreciated much more if Rand hadn't caught her half asleep on his porch.

Flushing, Jessamy explained her lack of manners. "I just ate, and the weather is so balmy, and I was so tired from the journey that I'm afraid I became quite drowsy."

Rand's voice revealed his amusement as he said, "That's all right. I think everyone should relax at Idlewood."

"A name that is quite appropriate, may I say," Jessamy put in, "for I have become idle this afternoon."

"You're entitled," was the easy response. Rand's mount shook its head in a noisy jangle of metal bit rings and curb chains, and he put an affectionate hand on the sorrel's velvety nose. "Shhh, Ulysses . . ."

"Ulysses?" Jessamy interrupted. "What a strange name for a horse!"

"Not at all," Rand answered, unperturbed. "He had gone from owner to owner when I got him, you know—from pillar to post—and now he's ended his travels."

"Really? Why would anyone choose to sell such a fine animal? Is he trouble?"

"Meaner than a snake," Rand said cheerfully, rubbing the stallion's nose. "But not to me."

"I see. He is very beautiful—"

"And so are you, Jessamy."

Caught off guard, Jessamy could only stare up at him with wide blue eyes. Another polite, insincere compliment? Or could he possibly have meant it?

"I trust your hats made it here in fine shape," Rand was saying casually, as if he had not just taken her by surprise.

"I . . . I don't know. I haven't unpacked my things yet, and my maid won't arrive until later."

"Do you like your room?"

After a moment's hesitation, Jessamy confessed, "I haven't even seen it yet. I have not been upstairs."

Amusement curled his mouth as Rand regarded her for a moment in silence. "You will like the room," he said confidently. "It was once my mother's."

Jessamy's mouth opened but no sound emerged. Idlewood was quite large enough to accommodate her in any room he chose, so if Rand had put her in his mother's chambers, he must think a great deal of her.

"I'm certain I shall like it," she murmured.

"I realize Idlewood may not hold a candle to Kenilworth, but it is considered one of the finest homes in Maryland at this time, though a bit *provincial*. Society may not be quite as grand or energetic in the country, but we manage."

"Don't misjudge me, Rand Montgomery. I am not a young girl in the first flush of womanhood who thinks of nothing but balls, soirées, and teas. I do have a smattering of knowledge about a few things besides silks, muslins, crepes, and who said what to whom." Jessamy's tone was censorious, her carriage stiff and unyielding as she faced him with a bold gaze.

"Did I say differently?" he returned.

"You implied otherwise, yes."

"Please accept my apologies." Rand swept her a mocking bow, curling the felt hat from his dark head in a graceful gesture, his eyes gleaming with amusement. His stallion snorted, jerking its head, and Rand tightened his grip on the reins, taking a step closer to say, "You must know that I have never considered you brainless for a moment, madam. On the contrary, I find you frighteningly intelligent."

Nonplussed, Jessamy muttered some inane comment that could scarcely have given credit to Rand's opinion; indeed, he must have thought her a complete ninnyhammer! To avoid an abrupt reversal of his opinion, she gathered her wits and straightened her spine, wafting her handpainted fan in a gentle motion to stir a slight breeze as she regarded him with a level gaze.

Rand's dark brows were lifted in that irritating gesture of amusement he affected, and his grin deepened. "You are most enlightening, madam," he said. "I shall look forward to our evening meal with bated breath. Until then . . . "

Accepting this with a reserved inclination of her fair head, Jessamy affected a pose as careless and studied as Rand's amusement, gazing with idle interest as he led his mount down the path to the stables. Her heartbeat belied her outward calm, however. She was not unaware of the honor done her by her placement in his mother's chambers, for she was not at all certain if she could bear the thought of just anyone inhabiting *her* parent's chambers. Yet it was an honor given with a backhanded compliment, for his manner was anything but admiring the majority of the time.

The sweet, lemony smell of magnolia blossoms rode a

fresh breeze, swirling an almost palpable fragrance around Jessamy as she rose from the rocking chair and entered the house. This journey was quickly becoming a battle of wits, and she was beginning to feel unarmed when it came to Rand Montgomery.

✳ Chapter 10 ✳

Shimmering rays of morning sunlight slanted through the wide-open window, illuminating the room. Jessamy cuddled deeper into her bed, sleepily contemplating the fact that the air was so much cooler and sweeter in the country than it was the city.

Wisps of mosquito netting—a necessity—stirred in graceful folds around the bed, a gauzy veil that diffused the early morning light. Birds warbled in heartrending song, and the air was thick and sweet with promise.

Surrendering to the inevitable, Jessamy sat up in the high, four-poster bed and swung her legs over the side. A small set of steps rested on the hooked rug beside the bed, and a porcelain bowl was tucked discreetly beneath the frame. Reaching for the dressing gown that was chastely disposed on a chair beside the bed, Jessamy slid into a pair of slippers while fastening the muslin wrap around her.

A pair of French doors beckoned, promising a splendid view of the garden from the vantage of the second-floor veranda. Yielding immediately, Jessamy crossed the room and swung wide the doors, stepping out into golden sunshine and a slice of Paradise. She almost expected to see a heavenly throne and bands of celestial angels hovering over the rose bushes and jasmine vines. How lovely it all was! She could hardly conceive of the fact that Rand Montgomery had engineered the building of the house and the arrangement of the gardens, but she had been assured of that fact at dinner the previous evening. He was a man of many talents, she mused.

A gurgle of childish laughter caught her attention, and she stepped close to the smooth length of railing, leaning out to see the source. Jessamy blinked in surprise at the sight of Chastity, the mystery boy Jimmy, and Rand cavorting upon the lawn like puppies. Her fingers curved around the white-painted railing, tightening. Who *was* the child? Rand was obviously fond of the boy, but then he seemed fond of Chastity also. For a man who professed to dislike children, he was full of contradictions.

So why, Jessamy mused as she retreated to her bedchamber, did Rand refuse to discuss Chastity's rightful inheritance with her? All her allusions to the reason for her visit to America had been met with stubborn resistance or light repartée. He would not seriously discuss Kenilworth, and she had been reluctant to force the issue. It was her belief that tact and patience usually accomplished so much more than coercion.

Sinking to the small stool in front of the dressing table, Jessamy picked up her favorite silver-backed hairbrush and began pulling it through her heavy mane of fine, pale hair, gazing thoughtfully at her reflection in the polished mirror. Perhaps she was wasting her time. It might be that Margaret was right in her opinion that she should just abandon the notion of Kenilworth's belonging to Chastity instead of the new earl. And dinner the evening before had been a rather stilted affair at best, with Rand being vague and pleasant, but quite uncommunicative.

"Perhaps I should just go home," she said aloud to her reflection, and was startled at the sound of her own voice. Perhaps she *should* go home.

An hour passed before Jessamy stood in the wide hall at the foot of the stairs, searching for Pauline. The thick maroon-and-gold carpet cushioned her steps as she passed the brocade settee with rolled arms and comfortable pillows. She paused in front of the gateleg table placed beneath a mirror to adjust a stray curl dangling in her eyes.

"Awake at last," a voice murmured dryly. Startled, she turned around to see Rand standing at the foot of the curved stairs.

"Yes. I am waiting on Wills and the others to arrive with the rest of my baggage."

"That may take weeks if they have to unload it for any reason. You seem to have a multitude of portmanteaus. Have you breakfasted this morning?"

Nodding, Jessamy replied, "Oh, yes. Polly brought me a tray with tea and muffins."

"Good." Rand fell into step beside her as Jessamy turned toward the French doors at one end of the long hall. "You may be pleased to learn that I am having a little social engagement this coming Saturday," he said conversationally. "It should be quite entertaining."

"Social engagement?"

"Yes, a picnic. This time of year I always put on a picnic for my neighbors in the county. It's rather a celebration, and most everyone will come. There will be tables and tables of food, so I am certain you will enjoy it."

Jessamy flashed him a sour glance. "How wonderful. I

am certain that I will. Will your Baltimore friends be in attendance also?''

''All my closest friends will be here,'' he answered, ''but there are very few from Baltimore.''

''I see,'' Jessamy said, though she did not see at all. Was Rand Montgomery two different people? One a man for the city, suave, debonair, and urbane, and the other a man for the country, more relaxed and casual? It certainly seemed that way.

''Mr. Montgomery,'' she began formally, ''I need to speak with you most urgently.''

''Certainly... supper tonight?''

''No, as soon as possible—immediately.''

Surprised by her intensity, Rand slanted her a narrow glance. ''Now?''

''That would be perfect.''

''Then let's walk in the garden while we talk,'' he suggested, taking her by one arm.

Inclining her head slightly, Jessamy gave him her arm without hesitation or comment, and they strolled across the veranda and out onto the brick-tiled path. Greek statues stood in graceful poses, and a large, Italian marble fountain trickled softly in one corner.

''Your gardens are lovely,'' she offered.

''Thank you. I planned them from a diagram my mother had. They're French in design.''

''Ah, I thought so. I saw similar gardens in France. But isn't it much larger than most with this design?''

''There are twenty-eight acres; quite a job to maintain, but my workers seem to enjoy it,'' Rand answered. ''Step this way,'' he directed then, ''there's another spot I think might interest you just beyond those far hedges.''

As she obeyed, Jessamy's skirts swung gracefully over

the tiled path bordered with sweet alyssum. Weeping willow branches drifted lazily in the breeze as they turned onto a much narrower path, and she could hear the faint rushing sound of running water.

"Is there a stream ahead?" she asked, and Rand nodded.

"A small one, but quite pretty, with smooth gray stones in the middle and hanging bushes to hide small children from grown-up eyes."

Jessamy smiled. "I remember hiding from Margaret when I was a little girl. I used to pretend I was a gnome or an elf, and that the curving branches of trees were my roof."

Faint lines of amusement bracketed Rand's mouth. "I was a pirate . . ."

"No!"

"Yes, and I hid in the leaf-coves to count my loot."

Laughing, Jessamy tried to picture Rand Montgomery as a youthful pirate and failed. "You seem more like the type to have been a Crusader," she teased.

"Oh, I had my own personal crusades, I can assure you," Rand returned easily. "Here we are. Watch your step . . ."

Words failed Jessamy for a moment as she looked up after stepping carefully over a small brick sticking up in the pathway. They were in a cemetery, with glistening white stones and cherubic monuments. Tall trees canopied the area like a loving mother watching over her children. Ivy and honeysuckle grew in wild profusion, twining around a white picket fence, and for an instant Jessamy was certain she had heard the laughter of children.

"Who . . ?" she began, but her half-asked question was answered by the sudden appearance of Chastity and Jimmy from behind a massive oak.

"Catch me!" Chastity called, racing across the lawn,

pink sashes flying behind her like bright banners, her gold curls in wild abandon. "Catch me if you can!"

Jimmy, his brown cheeks flushed red and his light eyes dancing with excitement, flashed behind her like a speeding arrow, clambering over the fence that circled the gravestones with an agility that was astounding.

Aghast at the sight of her usually immaculate daughter bearing grass stains on her pinafore, with her hair in a riot of tangles, Jessamy took pause.

"Perhaps they are gnomes or pirates," Rand suggested gently, and she turned her frowning gaze to his.

"Yes," she said, beginning to smile, "perhaps they are." And perhaps her discussion should wait until later.

Rand's hand under her elbow steered her along the path again, and they walked in companionable silence for a few steps. "Are all your family buried here?" she asked.

"My parents and my brothers are, and of course, those family retainers who wished to be interred with the others."

"Of course," she murmured. "Your two brothers died in the war, did they not?"

"Yes. I had stripes painted on the columns of my home to remind the world of their loss."

"But I thought there were only two brothers?" she questioned, frowning. "Aren't there stripes on three of the columns?"

"Yes," was the short reply. Rand led her to a tombstone near the fence. "The third column is for this relative who was killed in the war."

Puzzled, Jessamy looked from Rand's stiff face to the tombstone, and froze in shock. Her face must have shown the extent of her surprise, for Rand's arm moved to circle her back lightly, as if to hold her up.

She shook off his hold, and kneeling, Jessamy let her

fingers trace the name engraved on the stone, *James Matthew Peter Montgomery*. It had to be. No other Montgomery would have been given a name already in use—yet how did her husband, her Jamie, come to be buried in this cemetery so far from England without her knowing it?

Her shoulders shook and she could barely hear Rand's soft, astonished, "Did you not know, Jessamy?" Her head jerked from side to side, and Rand swore lightly under his breath. "I did not know you were unaware . . . I would never have just brought you without warning. Forgive me, Jessamy. I would never hurt you."

"No one ever told me how Jamie died, or where he was buried," she whispered in a choked voice. "The old earl, his father, was so grief stricken that he could not speak about it for a long time . . . and I never wanted to reopen old wounds."

Quietly kneeling on the grass beside her, Rand told her gently how he had written the earl to explain that his son Jamie had been brought to a field hospital near Idlewood, and that an officer who knew Rand had sent him a note saying he thought one of his relatives was there. It had indeed been a Montgomery, his own cousin, and when Jamie had died of his wounds shortly after Rand's arrival, he had had the body brought to the family plot. Rand did not tell Jessamy of the bitter conflict it had cost him to get Jamie's body to his home, how he had encountered a band of British soldiers who attacked him for his horses, and how he fought them off. It had been during that battle that Rand had suffered the long slash on his jaw.

Tears streamed down her face as Jessamy lifted her head to gaze at Rand. She stared at him blankly, having heard very little of what he'd said. "Why didn't you tell the earl this? We all thought our Jamie had been buried in a common grave. You should have told us!"

Startled, Rand recoiled. "But I did . . ."

Agitated, Jessamy stumbled to her feet, wiping grass from her skirts distractedly. Is this why he had brought her to this spot—to upset her so she would not confront him with Kenilworth and Chastity's inheritance? Did he think this would absolve him? Jessamy wiped at her tears, smearing grass across her cheeks while Rand stood in stunned silence.

"I had thought," he began after a moment, "that you would be pleased to know that your husband's body lay in a family plot. I see I was mistaken."

"Mummy!" Chastity called then, wedging herself between Rand and Jessamy, her eyes filled with laughter. "I beat Jimmy in a race, I did! He cannot run as fast as I!"

Staring at Rand, Jessamy ignored her daughter for the moment, saying, "Did you hope to distract me from my purpose, my lord? Did you think . . ?"

"It doesn't matter what I thought," Rand interjected quickly. "I can see you are in no state to converse on any level. If I had known of your ignorance on this, I would never have brought you here. We shall speak again as soon as you are able. Good day, madam."

"Mummy, are you angry with Uncle Rand?" Chastity asked, her youthful brow furrowed into lines as Rand pivoted on his heel and stalked away.

Clearing her throat, Jessamy managed to say, "No, not mad, pet. I . . . I was just sad."

"Because Daddy is here? Don't be sad, Mummy. Uncle Rand explained it all to me, and I'm not sad anymore. Daddy is in heaven now, where the sun always shines and it never rains unless you wish it to rain."

A tiny sob escaped Jessamy, and she clutched her child near, heedless of her grimy hands. "Did . . . did he say that?"

Chastity nodded. "Yes, and Jimmy told me that Uncle Rand buried Daddy with his daddy—isn't that right, Jimmy?"

The boy nodded solemnly, his large eyes fixed on Jessamy's face with a wary expression. Startled, she realized that the child must be Rand's nephew.

"Your father is buried here?" she asked him, and he nodded again, pointing to the marker engraved *Rolfe Allan Montgomery*. "Then that is your mother?" she asked, indicating the name *Morning Star* on the other side of the double marker. The child nodded again, obviously unwilling to speak to her. Poor boy. An orphan, left in the care of his uncle.

"And Uncle Rand got that scar on his cheek bringing Daddy to Idlewood, Mummy," Chastity was saying in a rapid chatter. "Bad soldiers wanted to take away his horses, but he would not let them."

"I see," Jessamy murmured, and this time she really did. She should not have flared up at Rand, should have remained calm instead of flying into a sulk. The true Rand Montgomery was beginning to emerge into a full picture of a man who was sensitive, yet bold; reserved, yet caring. Good God, she had seriously wronged him!

✳ Chapter 11 ✳

An apology, of course, was essential. Unfortunately, Rand did not appear willing to give Jessamy an opportunity to confront him in any capacity. He avoided Jessamy as energetically as possible. Jessamy had returned to the house after the scene in the cemetery to find Rand, words of sincere apology trembling on the tip of her tongue, but he was gone.

"Yes'm," Wills said solemnly, "he's done gone over to Mistah Wayne and Miss Selma's for a while." His gaze reflected sympathy as Jessamy just nodded, as if he knew that she was distressed.

The news struck deeply as she remembered that Wayne and Selma were Rand's true friends, and that he had gone to them for solace from her bitter, harsh words. Those words were impossible to retract now.

Resigned, Jessamy decided that she had no option but to wait until his return. Perhaps she could wait dinner on him, and hope somehow to mend the rift between them then. A hopeful smile curved her mouth as she ascended the graceful sweep of stairs to the second floor.

It was a quiet early-summer afternoon, the air heavy with the scent of new-mown grass, wild roses, and the sweet melody of birds chirruping in the willow trees. The sounds of summer drifted in Jessamy's open window as she sat before her dresser combing her unbound hair. It flowed in golden streams over her shoulders, framing her pensive face in gentle wisps as she gazed at her reflection.

Her best sprigged muslin should appeal to Rand with its simplicity, setting her features to advantage. But would he notice, or would he still be angry? Biting her lower lip between her teeth, she tugged at the comb one last time before winding her hair into a simple knot on her neck. He would listen to her apology. This was no light matter but a serious dilemma, which somehow had to reach an amicable solution. She and Rand could not continue like this. For a brief moment she considered returning home to England, then dismissed the thought just as quickly. She could not leave without Kenilworth securely in her daughter's possession.

Pushing back the scroll-carved dresser seat, she stood and gave herself a last inspection before leaving her chambers. The skirts of the muslin flowed in delicate wisps around her legs, moving with each step she took, and the nipped-in waist was definitely feminine with its pink satin sash. Jessamy's thoughts turned to Rand as she stepped into the wide hallway.

She was surprised to find him sitting at the table when she arrived. As she entered the dining room, he rose from his chair and bowed in her general direction—a polite, meaningless action.

"I see that your sentiments have not impaired your appetite," he murmured cynically, and Jessamy stiffened.

She was fully aware of the *sentiments* he referred to, and noted bitterly that he seemed to have regained his customary sardonic composure.

"Rarely do I lose my appetite," she returned sweetly, "*remember*?" This conversation was definitely not beginning in the manner she had hoped.

"Ah yes, I do seem to recall," he mocked. "I had not thought to forget such an unusual appetite in a woman, but it seems I had."

A footman seated her, and Jessamy shook out her folded linen napkin and placed it across her lap neatly, smoothing the edges with her fingers, anything to keep from having to look at him for a few moments—anything to keep from having to meet his eyes, those eyes which seemed to see into her soul at times.

The tantalizing aroma of chicken teased her, wafting from the butler's pantry into the dining area, but for once Jessamy could not summon an appetite. Indeed, the thought of food at this moment was repugnant. Glancing up, she caught Rand's eyes resting upon her curiously, and she attempted a smile.

"I was hoping to—" she began, intending to apologize, but Rand interrupted.

"To talk?" His voice was harsh and cutting as he said, "I am sick to death of *talk*, dear lady."

Tensing, Jessamy shot back defensively, "But why, my lord, when you are so expert at idle talk?"

"Idle?" His mouth curved in a mocking smile. "Perhaps, but not nearly as expert as you, dear Lady Jessamy. You English are quite proficient in meaningless conversation, from what I've observed."

"Thank you."

This could only deteriorate rapidly if continued, so Jessamy attempted to divert the topic of conversation to one less volatile. "Did you have a pleasant visit with the Copleys? I was told that you had gone there."

"I did."

"And how is Selma Copley?" she tried again, reaching blindly for her glass of water. "Well, I hope?"

"She looked . . . quite well . . . to me." Now Rand's smile was decidedly nasty, but she refused to rise to the bait.

"Well, I'm pleased that a visit with your friends can restore your pleasant mood," she said.

"Yes. Good company seems to do that for me." Rand glanced over his shoulder as if looking for a diversion, then returned his attention to Jessamy. Silence stretched between them for several long moments as each strove for something to say.

Finally Jessamy began, "I was hoping that I might have an opportunity to apologize this evening—"

"No apology is necessary," he cut in.

"I disagree. I was extremely insensitive, and my distress cannot excuse that."

Rand's eyes met hers, but before he could speak the door from the short hall attached to the butler's pantry swung open to admit Pauline to the dining room.

"Well!" the housekeeper said triumphantly, her dark eyes gleaming, "I am shore glad to see both of you settin' at the same table again!" Her mouth stretched in a wide, white smile. "It does my ole heart good."

Narrowing his eyes, Rand muttered, "I knew that I should have kept you to the kitchen, Polly. You try to run me like you run my house."

Unabashed, Polly chuckled hugely. "You're right about

that, Mistah Rand! But I has a lot less trouble runnin' the kitchen than I does runnin' you! There's a heap less trouble in the kitchen, and a powerful lot of trouble goin' on out here! At least in the kitchen, the food don' talk back!''

Jessamy's lips twitched, then she broke into a helpless laugh at Rand's futile attempt to hide his amusement. There was an understanding between master and servant that had nothing at all to do with servitude, but was more one of affection and tolerance. It was part of the family atmosphere one could feel throughout Idlewood.

''Since we are speaking about food,'' Rand admonished Polly, ''why don't you explain that tempting aroma that has been tormenting me for several minutes.''

''Chicken pot pie!'' Polly declared, hands on her ample hips. ''My specialty, and Miss Jessamy's favorite!''

''How did you know?'' Jessamy asked, laughing. ''When I was a child I used to crave the pies Cook would make for me.''

''I can well believe that,'' Rand mocked softly, cocking a dark brow in her direction as Jessamy bristled.

''Now, don't you two go to fussin' again,'' Polly scolded, wagging a finger at them. ''I done gone to too much trouble fixin' you up this good supper for you to ruin it! I'll bring it in.''

Swinging about with a rustle of taffeta petticoats beneath her wide cotton skirts, Polly bustled back into the butler's pantry, muttering beneath her breath. Neither Rand nor Jessamy could quite understand her sentences, though an occasional word such as ''foolish'' or ''bird-witted'' filtered back to them.

This time the silence that descended was comfortable, and Rand and Jessamy regarded one another without animosity. A crystal decanter of wine stood on the sideboard, and Rand indicated it with a wave of his hand.

"Would you care for some wine?" he asked pleasantly, and she nodded.

"Please."

Without waiting for a servant, Rand rose from his chair and crossed to the carved rosewood sideboard. Crystal tinkled musically as he pulled the stopper and poured wine into fragile-stemmed glasses. Once his gaze lifted to regard Jessamy, and she felt a sudden warmth flood her at the expression in his eyes. Was she blushing like a young miss still in the schoolroom? she wondered in horror. Dear God, she hoped not!

"Thank you," she murmured when Rand held out her wine-glass. Jessamy took a quick sip, letting the cool, pale liquid flow down her throat as she began to relax.

"I think we should declare a truce," Rand said with a short laugh as he returned to his chair across from hers, "or Polly will become more than a little miffed at us. She's quite particular about her meals, you may have discovered. And when she is irritated, she always finds some way of letting you know. She has a very sneaky manner of exacting revenge."

Jessamy had the thought that Rand should know quite a bit about that himself, but she held her tongue. Why begin the argument all over again?

The steaming chicken pie was brought in on a silver tray garnished with slices of fresh vegetables and fruit. The crusty top of the pastry had been brushed with butter and was so flaky that it appeared to have been made of a hundred tiny layers. Thick broth oozed from steaming cuts in the crust, and the pie was filled with big chunks of chicken, potatoes, carrots, and peas.

It grew quiet in the dining room as Jessamy reveled in her huge slabs of chicken pie, ignoring most of the other dishes Polly had prepared. Rand watched her with amusement, wondering how she could eat so much when she was so small. He had finished his portion and was awaiting dessert before Jessamy began her third helping.

Glancing up, she found his thoughtful gaze resting on her and asked, "Is there something amiss?"

He shook his head and answered, "No, I was just thinking of this morning—in the cemetery." His frown deepened. "It seems that your father-in-law spared you my letter, for reasons unknown."

Sensing how difficult it was for him to bring the matter up again, Jessamy said softly, "I truly never knew about your letter, believe me."

"Oh, I do. Now that I know the truth, your reaction makes much more sense to me." Rand pushed his empty plate aside before an alert servant could spring forward to remove it, and leaned his elbows on the table, clenching his hands and regarding her seriously. "I can understand your anger this morning."

Sighing, Jessamy related, "I was so shocked at seeing Jamie's name here, at Idlewood. When he went off to fight that August of 1814, he was so excited. He was to land in the Chesapeake Bay area with four thousand other brave British soldiers, I found out later."

"Yes. The Bladensburg races," Rand said, referring to the invaders who had poured across Maryland, entered the capital city, and set fire to most of the public buildings, including the Capitol building and the White House.

"Races?" Jessamy echoed, confused. "Oh, you mean . . . then Jamie died soon after . . . ?" She paused, needing confirmation but unable to complete her sentence.

"Jamie Montgomery died not far from here, Jessamy."

It had been years since her husband's death, and after the shock of seeing his grave, Jessamy had few tears left to shed. There would always be sorrow and regret, but her grief had mellowed with time.

"But—but how did you find him? How did you know about Jamie?" she asked.

"I told you earlier, remember?" he reminded gently, and Jessamy nodded.

"Oh yes—something about a field hospital."

"Actually, it was more of a tent," Rand said wryly.

"Did you . . . were you able to speak with Jamie before . . . before he . . . "

"Died? Yes, he was weak, but still able to talk to me."

Jessamy's heart fluttered and her mouth was so dry she took a quick swallow of water. Jamie. Jamie and Rand had met, had spoken to one another, and she hadn't known it all these years, had thought that he'd died alone in a foreign country with no family for comfort.

Sensing her thoughts, Rand said softly, "He spoke of you, his 'dear Jessamy' and 'darling baby Chastity,' his two sweet girls. He did not fear death, but hated the thought of leaving you and Chastity behind . . . "

"Oh, Rand, how I wish I had known before!" In spite of her resolve, Jessamy's eyes misted. "Did Jamie suffer?"

"No, not at the last." He saw no need in telling her the details, which could only be distressing to a woman unfamiliar with the ways of war.

"Then you were with him when he died?"

"I was with him until almost the very last moment. I recalled my father's death, and how he wanted his family with him, just as Jamie wanted you to be there. I could not leave him alone to die without family or comfort, Jessamy.

And after it was over, when he was at peace, I felt compelled to bring him to Idlewood to bury him in the garden with Jimmy's parents."

"Jimmy's parents?" Jessamy recalled that the boy's parents had also died during the war, leaving him an orphan and left to the care of his uncle. "War destroys families, doesn't it?" she murmured.

"Yes. Wars always do."

"It was good of you to take Jimmy in the way you have."

"He is my brother's son, and content with me though he would rather be with his mother's people at times," Rand said dryly. "Every time I leave for Baltimore he runs back to the forests."

"Yet he seems happy."

"He's as happy as a lad without parents can be."

Jessamy caught the rough edge in Rand's tone, and sensed his bitterness about the recent war.

"Yes. Chastity feels a loss as well," Jessamy said.

"War is never easy, but sometimes necessary, Lady Jessamy. We all pay a high price for what we believe."

"And you believed this war was necessary?"

"Very necessary. It was as important in its own way as the *first* war for independence."

"How patriotic . . . "

"True. I am a man who loves his country."

Jessamy's color receded, and she stared at him in dismay. It seemed that Rand was a part of that small percentage of the American population that fed off the war's renewed feelings of nationalism. That meant she could never fit into his world.

"I'm tired," she said suddenly when he gazed at her quizzically, and she managed to smile. Her head was beginning to pound dreadfully, and she wanted to forget the tangle she had created with her need to possess Kenilworth for Chastity.

Wills promptly appeared to pull back her chair, and she rose from the table, as did Rand. He bowed politely, his eyes meeting hers for a brief instant.

"I bid you good evening, fair lady," Rand said, taking her hand between his. "Rest well."

"Thank you," Jessamy returned, caught up in the feeling that Rand was disturbed by her presence at Idlewood. It was more than a feeling—it was a certainty.

✳ Chapter 12 ✳

Idlewood buzzed with busy plans for the upcoming picnic, which was to last for two days. Visitors came from miles around, and since the distance was usually great, they remained as guests for the weekend. Pauline's voice could be heard throughout the house, echoing the sounds of detailed orders to the other servants.

At least, Jessamy thought gloomily, the atmosphere had lightened considerably. Since that day in the cemetery the house had been hushed and quiet, with even the servants sensing the strain between Rand and Jessamy. Jessamy could feel everyone avoiding her as though it was her fault that Rand and she were having such difficulties. Even Chastity had protested Rand's absence from the house all day long.

Sighing, she turned to the oval cheval mirror and inspected her appearance before joining the party downstairs. Why did she even care about Rand's opinion? she asked herself, then immediately answered her own question. Because she cared about Rand Montgomery. Oh, not in the same affectionate way she had cared about her poor Jamie; after all, the marriage had been one of convenience. Jessamy had come to care about Rand in a much deeper way that threatened to ruin all her plans.

Jessamy stared at her reflection, barely recognizing the composed woman in a gown of pale green. She looked the part of an English lady, with her quilled lace and mint satin ribbons, the gored skirt dropping in a bell shape and vandyked in several flounces, yet she felt very much like an awkward schoolmiss at this moment.

Bending, Jessamy picked up her M. Danys fan with its depiction of a stylish English lady on the parchment folds. It would be hot today, even in the garden, and already she could hear the soft strains of music and the laughing chatter of guests drifting up the curved staircase to her room. It was time to put on her "social" face and mingle with the crowd.

One hand grazed the smooth oak of the balustrade as she descended the graceful swoop of stairs to the first floor. Bright swathes of color lay before her like a bouquet of fresh spring flowers as the women moved about in their gaily colored dresses.

"Jessamy!"

Turning, Jessamy saw Corinne Blackwell moving toward her with a bright smile, dark hair bouncing in curls on each side of her gamin face.

"Corinne, I did not realize you were already here."

"Yes, isn't this fun? I do so love Rand's picnics! They are always so gay and lighthearted, and I have such a wonderful time."

"You are staying all day?" Jessamy asked, suddenly feeling the need for friendly company, and Corinne reminded her very much of Melinda Fielding, one of her dearest and oldest friends in England.

"Oh, yes! Because we have to travel so far we always stay the weekend, like some of the others."

Nodding, Jessamy murmured, "Yes, we do that at home, also."

Tucking her hand into the crook of Jessamy's elbow, Corinne began to thread her way through the crowd, saying with a mischievous smile, "Tell me about you and Rand."

"Rand?" she echoed blankly. "Why, there's nothing to tell, Corinne."

"Nonsense! You can talk to me," Corinne coaxed. "I can be quite discreet when I must."

"I don't know what you mean . . . "

"Oh fiddlesticks, Jessamy! Why, it's all over Baltimore county that Rand Montgomery is simply mad about you! Why else would he have brought you to his home when it would have been much simpler to leave you in the city? Now, do tell me . . . "

Bewildered, Jessamy grasped the opportunity for silence provided by the appearance of a servant with a tray of drinks. Blindly she reached out to grasp the first goblet she saw. She gulped its contents, earning a wide-eyed gaze from Corinne.

"Be careful," the brunette beauty advised, "that's a mint julep, which has the same effect as a glass of champagne."

"Let's go outside," Jessamy said in a strangled voice, feeling the immediate need for fresh air.

"Are you well?"

"I just need some fresh air."

Reaching the veranda, which was crowded with tables and chairs for the guests, Jessamy took a deep breath. The pungent odor of roasting pig permeated the air, drifting from the huge brick pits dug just beyond the garden. An outside dance floor had been laid for those so inclined, and white-uniformed servants milled about the grounds with silver trays bearing chilled beverages. Long buffet tables had been set up, and platters of food were watched over by young black girls with long fans of bamboo to keep away any insects.

Smiling and nodding, Jessamy was introduced to a multitude of guests, people who had been Rand Montgomery's friends and neighbors for years and were avidly curious about the lovely Englishwoman who was visiting. She fielded questions that were polite and not so polite, leveling what the old earl had once referred to as a "stone fence look" on those rude enough to ask about her relationship with Rand.

"See what I mean?" Corinne whispered in her ear after one particularly persistent old lady demanded to know if Jessamy was the young gel who had come to snare the prize match of Baltimore. "People are wondering."

"Well, let them continue to wonder!" Jessamy retorted with feeling. "My relationship with Rand Montgomery is not for public conjecture . . ."

"*Au contraire*," a smooth masculine voice said in her ear. "Public conjecture cannot be ruled, my lady."

Jessamy turned to Rand, eyeing him narrowly, while Corinne tapped him on the arm with her folded fan.

"You!" Corinne said playfully. "You know how all these people love to talk. I imagine that's a universal trait, and not one peculiar to Americans only, wouldn't you agree, Jessamy?"

"Of course. I just find it distasteful." Jessamy gave Corinne a silent salute of thanks for giving her a moment to gather her wits, then said to Rand, "There is quite a turnout for your affair. Even the weather has cooperated."

"It always does," he said imperturbably, a twinkle in his dark eyes as he regarded Jessamy.

She was well aware of what a fine picture he made in his dark coat of superfine, his snowy cravat, and the fawn trousers that fit him like a glove. He appeared every inch the master of Idlewood, regal and handsome. It suddenly, painfully, occurred to her that Rand would look quite impressive as the Earl of Wemyess, master of Kenilworth.

Looking up, Jessamy caught an expression of awareness in Corinne's eyes, and knew the brunette had sensed her thoughts. Nothing would do but to smile, to erase any impression that she might be longing after such a personage as Rand Montgomery, who was, everyone declared, the undisputed "catch" of Baltimore county.

"Of course," Jessamy said gaily, "the weather would hardly deny all these guests a grand time! I should have known you would take care of all the loose ends, Mr. Montgomery."

"Yes, you certainly should have," he agreed. "Come with me, Jessamy. I have someone I would very much like for you to meet. Will you join us, Corinne?"

He held out his hand and Jessamy could hardly refuse it with any grace, though her heart was fluttering like the wings of a trapped bird. Slender fingers were enclosed in his warm grasp as he led her to a man sitting alone close to the fountain. Jessamy's breath caught as the man looked up at them with bleary eyes, and at the same time she saw the empty trouser leg and wooden crutch. Her eyes flew to Rand, but he was gazing down at the man intently.

"Wayne," he said softly, "I would like to introduce you to my cousin . . . "

Lurching to a stand with his crutch, Wayne Copley focused his eyes on Jessamy with belligerence. Corinne drew closer, flanking Jessamy's other side as if for protection, and Wayne's eyes moved to her.

"' 'Lo, C'rinne," he slurred. "How ya doin'?"

"Wayne," Corinne said with a bright smile, "this is Lady Jessamy Montgomery. She is Rand's cousin here from . . ."

"I know where she's from," Wayne snapped. He hobbled closer, his face mere inches from Jessamy's and his breath sour with whisky. "Whatcha think of America—what's left of it after the British got through tryin' to burn it down?"

Flicking a glance toward Rand, half expecting him to interfere, Jessamy managed to mutter, "I like it . . ."

"Like it, do you? That's fine and dandy, but I don't accept it. Why'd you come over here anyway—to marry Rand?"

Cheeks flaming, Jessamy's glance at Rand was beseeching, but he didn't take the hint. He was gazing at his drunken friend with compassion, and his tone was gentle when he said, "That's enough, Wayne. I think you need to lie down and rest for a while."

Nodding numbly, Wayne accepted Rand's arm, leaning heavily on him. He paused to look directly at Jessamy. "Go home, English . . ."

Jessamy, silent and appalled, felt Corinne's arm tighten around her waist as the pair moved slowly off.

"Don't pay any attention to him," Corinne said. "He is a miserable man when he's in his cups. It's his war injuries that have left him so bitter, I think. That and the fact that Highland, the Copley estate, was burned to the ground by the British during the war. He's never accepted the fact that the war is over."

Hot tears burned Jessamy's eyelids, but she refused to let them fall. "Does . . . does Rand think the same way?" she asked brokenly, then added, "Never mind. I know he does."

"No! No, Jessamy, that's not true! Why, Rand doesn't think that at all."

"Yes he does. He can't even defend me, and I am certain it is because he feels the way Wayne Copley does about the war and England. He has just tried to be nice to me because I am a guest in his home."

"No, don't you see? Wayne is his best friend, and has been since they were children. That's why he didn't defend you. And besides, the war hurt everyone, American *and* British. I'm just glad it's over and that we can be friends, Jessamy."

Jessamy managed a wan smile. "I am, too, Corinne, but I think it's time I went home."

"Home?" Corinne echoed.

"Yes. Home to England, where I belong. I don't belong here. Why, these people are just being nice to me for Rand's sake, because he belongs here." Jessamy passed a hand over her eyes. "I'm an outsider, and even if I don't accomplish what I came for, I'm going home."

Idlewood rocked with the news of Jessamy's imminent departure. Servants whispered behind their hands, saddened that the English lady and her child would be leaving, while Jessamy's staff gave heartfelt sighs of relief at the news. Though Margaret was relieved, she knew how distressed Chastity would be, and dreaded telling her.

In the end, it was Jessamy who told the child as gently as possible, and, as expected, she took it hard, pleading with her mother to be allowed to stay. "Or let's take Jimmy back with us!" Chastity added when her pleas were to no avail. "He gets so lonesome here, and when Uncle Rand goes back into the city, Jimmy often goes to live in the woods with his mother's people."

"I don't think he'd be happy in England," Jessamy said, "but perhaps Uncle Rand can bring him for a visit one day."

And Rand Montgomery was the last person she told of her intentions, determinedly cornering him in his study.

"Please be seated while I finish this letter to the supervisor of my warehouses," Rand instructed pleasantly, his pen scrawling across the parchment in firm, precise strokes. "I'll be with you in a moment."

Seating herself in the wingbacked chair across from him, Jessamy waited with an impatiently swinging foot, something she rarely did. It was a sign of bad breeding to exhibit impatience, but she found it increasingly difficult to control. Finally she cut through the stony silence in the room.

"I'm leaving Idlewood."

Rand looked up in surprise, frowned, and put down his pen. "May I ask where you are going?"

"Home."

"To England?"

"Yes, that is where my home is," she answered with asperity.

"Don't be precipitate, Jessamy. I do not have a ship going to England now, and you and Chastity cannot just leave Maryland on such short notice."

"I can stay at the Baltimore residence until arrangements can be made," she pointed out.

"No." His brow furrowed into deep lines. "Why this sudden urge to return to England? Was it something I said or did? The scene in the cemetery, perhaps? I only meant . . . "

"No, that's not it, Rand. I would like to apologize again for misunderstanding your motives that day in the cemetery, so I will do so now. I am truly sorry that I lost control of myself and made cruel remarks. It was unforgivable."

"Then why are you leaving—because Wayne Copley insulted you yesterday? Not everyone feels that way, and I understand that you were deeply distressed by his remarks."

"Yes, but I understood his feelings. I was foolish to come here at all, thinking that I could . . . could change your mind about Kenilworth. I can't." Jessamy stood and gazed down at Rand with mixed emotions. "My maids are packing my things now. I should like to leave as soon as possible."

"Very well," Rand said, "but I would like you to allow me to arrange your passage on one of my ships. I would feel better knowing that you and Chastity would be on a well-run, sound vessel."

Jessamy agreed for Chastity's sake, thinking that perhaps a few more days would give the child time to adjust to the idea of returning to England and leaving her new-found friends.

The few days passed quickly, much more quickly than she had realized they would, and Jessamy was surprised by the feelings of regret which haunted her nights. In her entire life, she had never yielded on a point that she felt was right, but she was giving up now. Kenilworth would be Rand's and go to his heirs, not Chastity. She had lost.

On the day that the landau pulled up in front of Idlewood to take them into Baltimore, Jessamy was astonished to see Rand Montgomery having his luggage loaded onto the wagon that would follow.

"Are you going with us to Baltimore?" she asked.

"That I am, madam," was Rand's casual answer.

"There's no need, though I certainly appreciate your thoughtfulness—" she began.

But he cut her off to say, "I'm not going just to Baltimore. I am traveling to England with you."

Jessamy stared. "England?"

"Yes—England."

✳ Chapter 13 ✳

The trip from Baltimore to London took two weeks longer than the passage to Baltimore had taken, and Jessamy—who never experienced seasickness—had come uncomfortably close to being sick during the voyage. Rand had behaved with distant courtesy the entire duration, so that by the time they reached London she was almost glad to see the last of him for a while. The tension had been entirely too wearing on her frayed nerves.

Jessamy and Chastity were to travel to Kenilworth, while he would stay the winter in London, an arrangement which suited her perfectly. She much preferred keeping the inevitable at bay for as long as possible.

Autumn in the country was beautiful, and the familiar sights of Kenilworth were even more precious to her now, when she knew that at any moment Rand could take them away from her. Jessamy dreaded what the post would bring all winter, wondering when the axe would fall, severing her and Chastity from Kenilworth forever.

When the letter finally came in the spring, it was not an

announcement of Rand's intentions to take over the estates, but a summons to London.

"What do you think he means, my lady?" Margaret asked in a troubled tone. "Why are we to open up the townhouse in the city—doesn't the earl have his own? After all, it's hardly as if he has no money."

"I don't know, Margaret. He will more than likely explain when we arrive, but I suggest that he intends to claim his inheritance soon."

"Oh dear! Then why aren't you perturbed?" she wanted to know. "I would have thought you would be more upset, but you are so calm . . ."

Jessamy smiled. "I've been expecting this, and I do not intend to go down without protest."

Margaret's eyes narrowed. "What are you planning, Jessamy?" she demanded in much the same tone she had used when Jessamy was a small girl.

"I've had all winter to think, Margaret, and I believe I have worked out a scheme that will influence the earl's decision about Kenilworth."

"Oh, dear me! Do not, I pray, utter another word!" Margaret begged, throwing up her hands. "It is just too bad of you to torment me like this."

Jessamy's smile reminded her old nurse of a cat's, and she had a distinctly wicked gleam in her eyes that boded no good for the new earl's plans to possess Kenilworth.

"Shall we begin packing?" Jessamy said. "I would like to be in London as soon as possible."

The Season in London officially commenced each April with the performance of the opera. Of course, most of the *ton* had arrived in the city from their country estates many weeks prior, opening up their houses, seeing to new wardrobes, and gathering all the latest tidbits of gossip. Jessamy was no exception.

Though she'd had a later start, she looked forward to three exciting months of social activities. Rand Montgomery, it seemed, had already made himself the talk of the *ton* with his casual manners and exceedingly good looks. Jessamy listened to the gossip with polite attention, then changed the subject as rapidly as possible. For some reason, it bothered her to think of Rand as a very eligible man.

The work on the townhouse took up more of her time than she'd planned, what with removing dust covers, repairing the stable and carriage house, restocking the kitchen, and the hundred other little details that required time and thought. The skeleton staff that had been left to care for the house had been limited in what they could accomplish, and as they were some of the old earl's most loyal retainers, and most quite elderly, Jessamy had a formidable task in righting the household. She had quite deftly arranged matters so no feelings would be hurt, and the work was soon done.

With all the household tasks accomplished, she turned to the important matter of her wardrobe. Mme. DuPont was the most popular modiste of the day, and to be seen in one of her creations gave an aura of prestige to any aspiring debutante. While Jessamy debated the wisdom of parting with the extraordinary funds required to finance sartorial splendor, she received in the morning post a short letter and a bank draft from Rand, which she was instructed to use in the acquiring of new gowns.

"Why do you think he did that?" Margaret mused aloud.

"So I don't embarrass him, I imagine," Jessamy retorted dryly. "After all, has he bothered to visit us in the week that we've been here? No. We haven't seen or heard from him until now, so he undoubtedly believes that I will dress as a drudge and embarrass him in some way.''

"How could he even consider that you might, when he complained so heartily about your gowns and petticoats in Baltimore?'' Margaret pointed out. ''No, the earl has some other reason in mind, I am certain.''

"Well, all that aside, nothing is going to spoil my season in London,'' Jessamy said firmly. She would have ball gowns, opera cloaks, carriage dresses, riding outfits, walking dresses, shoes, half-boots, reticules, gloves, and stockings—and she would enjoy herself to the fullest.

In only a few weeks, Jessamy had her quota of clothing. She was not surprised when another missive came from Rand in the morning post, this one extending an invitation to the opera for herself and Margaret. While Jessamy was delighted, Margaret was beside herself with excitement.

"The opera! Oh my, what a most charming man to think of me! I have never been to the opera, as you well know, and I had not ever dreamed that I might have this opportunity...''

"Margaret,'' Jessamy said dryly, ''please contain yourself. The object of going to the opera is to see and be seen, so you must now obtain a suitable gown. Let us send for Mme. Dupont immediately.''

"Oh, I simply cannot believe that the earl has asked me to go with you—do you think I should, dear? I should hate to be just a bother, or feel as if I am in the way.''

"Nonsense! I would feel much more comfortable with Rand Montgomery if you were there as a buffer between us. Please do not cry off, Margaret.''

"Very well, dear. Especially as you know how excited I

am at the prospect of the opera.'' Margaret clapped her hands together and gave a happy sigh. ''What a dear, *dear* man the earl is!''

Jessamy's eyes narrowed. ''Now, let us not go into raptures over this. The earl is the same man he always was, but he has just had the courtesy and grace to include us in an invitation that has probably lingered upon his desk for weeks. I set no store by this, and neither should you.''

Easier said than done, Jessamy reflected silently, willing her thoughts from Rand Montgomery to the opera.

Jessamy was the perfect picture of a classic English beauty with her pale blond hair and creamy complexion. Her cheeks were flushed with excitement, her blue eyes sparkling. To Margaret's consternation, she wore a low-cut gown of pale peach watered silk over a cream foile slip, but appeased her old nurse's sensibilities by adding a lace cape with tiny pearl buttons for modesty. Milky pearls were twisted in the heavy braids that were neatly coiled at the back of her neck, and a single strand of diamonds and pearls graced her slender neck. She was, Margaret and Chastity declared in almost the same breath, a vision of beauty.

But if Rand Montgomery shared their opinion, he certainly failed to mention it. Nor did his face betray any admiration or displeasure. His bland expression could have been directed toward any of his acquaintances as he asked to see Chastity. Though she was pleased that he wished to see her daughter, Jessamy could not help a twinge of irritation that he had not even noticed her appearance.

After nearly a half hour of listening to Rand read from

one of Chastity's favorite storybooks, Jessamy suggested, "I think we should leave now, before the opera is over."

Rand's brow rose and he said politely, "I promised to read her the letter I received from Jimmy, then we shall leave."

It was another quarter hour before the letter was read and Chastity had been tucked in for the night, which made them arrive at the Opera House when the curtain had already risen. Boxes at the King's Theater, also known as the Royal Italian Opera House, were sold on a subscription basis for as much as 2,500 pounds for the season, and were filled night after night with gorgeous, bejeweled ladies of the highest rank. The Duchess of Richmond and the Duchess of Argyll, Lady Melbourne and Lady Jersey were among the box holders, as well as the Prince Regent himself and the royal Dukes of Cumberland and Gloucester.

The King's Theater in Haymarket was London's most fashionable center of entertainment. The huge horseshoe-shaped auditorium held five tiers of boxes, a gallery, and a pit, and was large enough to hold 3,300 persons. Admission to the pit cost dearly, and was usually filled with fops and dandies who made a great nuisance of themselves during the performance, strolling about to show off their new garments, rattling their ivory-headed canes and the lids to their enameled snuff boxes, and chattering loudly to one another without being affected in the slightest when people in the gallery shouted at them to be quiet.

Rand was amused by all the hullaballoo, Jessamy—as she had often attended the opera—was bored, and Margaret was enthralled.

"But I can't understand a word of it," she whispered to Jessamy after they were seated. "What is she saying?"

"The opera is in Italian," Jessamy explained. "That is

Madame Pasta, who just made her London debut last year and is now a success in Bellini's *Norma*. Tonight she is portraying Cherubino in *Le Nozze di Figaro*. My Italian is not very fluent, or I could translate more easily for you.''

''Don't they ever sing in proper English?'' Margaret asked, rather disgruntled by this revelation.

''Sometimes, but usually only at Covent Garden, Drury Lane, and other unlicensed theaters on the fringe of the central city,'' Rand answered for Jessamy, his tone revealing how amused he was by Margaret's naïve question.

Jessamy slid Rand a glance, thinking how handsome he was in his perfectly tailored suit from Bond Street. Indeed, it was extremely difficult for her to concentrate upon the opera and Madame Pasta's remarkable voice, for Rand Montgomery was entirely too distracting. Even the sight of the Prince Regent's portly frame in the next box did not divert her attention from Rand, but poor Margaret almost swooned with excitement.

Indeed, the opera was all Margaret could discuss for the next two days, while Jessamy brooded over the fact that Rand had hardly acknowledged her existence during the entire evening. He had been polite—and distant.

So, on the second day after the opera, when a footman informed Sara, Jessamy's personal maid, that the Earl of Wemyess was waiting in the small parlor after requesting an audience with Lady Montgomery, she hurried to change into a more presentable gown, wondering what had precipitated his visit. She didn't have to wonder long, for after she descended the curved stairs and received his warm, sincere compliment that she looked quite ravishing, Rand came directly to the point.

"I have come to beg a boon, Jessamy," he said, seating her in a cushioned chair in the parlor.

"A boon?" she echoed. "And what favor can I possibly do for you?"

"I need an escort," he said promptly.

"An escort?" she repeated, beginning to feel very much like a parrot. "I mean . . . why do you need an escort?"

"I find that I must attend one of those dreary little affairs at Almack's or risk offending Lady Jersey—which would not do at all—and so I am begging you to attend with me. Will you do it?"

"Ah, I see. You need a protectress, not an escort, is that what you're trying not to say?"

Rand's grin dazzled her for a moment, and his dark eyes crinkled with amusement. "You are very perceptive," he approved.

"Yes, I daresay I am."

"Then you will go?"

Jessamy managed a smile, though she rather wished she could stamp on his foot instead. How dare he invite her to be his companion just so he would not have all those young debutantes thrown at him by their mamas? It was the outside of enough to have her feelings for him ignored, and one day she would lose control of her temper and tell him so.

But now all she said was, sweetly, "Of course, I will attend Almack's with you, my lord. It promises to be quite entertaining. Shall I practice pugilism in case some overexcitable young female actually attacks you? Or perhaps I should hire a bodyguard . . . "

"Your sarcasm is showing," Rand reprimanded. "Do you find it amusing that I have a horde of anxious mamas tossing their horse-faced daughters at my head? I, for one, do not find it amusing in the least."

"It's one of the perils of being an earl, my lord. You are supposed to enjoy it."

"Well, I do not. I prefer ladies of my own choice, thank you."

Hesitating, Jessamy asked as if the answer did not matter in the least, "And have you been able to find many ladies of your own choice?"

Now he shot her a curious glance. "Why do you ask that? Do you have some likely candidates in mind also?"

"Oh, no. I am not a marriage mart, thank you. When are we to go to Almack's dreary festivities?"

"Tomorrow evening. I shall arrive promptly at seven in order to fetch you up, so do try to be ready on time."

"I am always punctual." Jessamy defended herself, bridling at the earl's superior tone. "If I remember correctly—which I do—*you* were the one who made us late to the opera."

Rand's eyes gleamed with amusement. "Yes, I believe you must be right—for once. But I shall be on time tomorrow night. Until then, Lady Jessamy." He bowed over her hand with all the skill and grace of an accomplished courtier, and took his leave.

Jessamy, gazing down at the back of the hand he had just kissed, wondered if she didn't much prefer the rather rough-clad man in buckskins to this new, distant dandy who was continually in attendance at routs, teas, soirées and the like. She had even heard about his fondness for the gaming hells, where it was said he was quite proficient at whist, faro, and hazard. And of course he was an excellent whip, with fine-blooded horses that were the envy of many of the *ton*. It was said that he had actually been invited to be a member of the Four-in-hand Club, whose membership was closely guarded, and the gossips whispered that Rand was well favored by Beau Brummell, having been invited to sit with him in the bow window at White's.

Jessamy's eyes narrowed, and she wondered with a sense of frustration if Rand courted her favor for herself or for her daughter. Not that she was envious of his preference for her child; indeed, she was grateful that he shared her high opinion of Chastity, but Jessamy greatly would have liked to know exactly where his intentions were aimed . . .

✳ Chapter 14 ✳

Almack's was a popular assembly hall in King Street frequented by all the *ton*. Procuring vouchers from Lady Jersey or Lady Cowper was not a matter easily accomplished, as attendance was closely regulated. To be excluded from Almack's meant certain death to one's social aspirations.

Almack's brought back bittersweet memories for Jessamy as she recalled her own coming-out. Though the Connor family was of excellent lineage and breeding, her father's estates had been encumbered due to a failing of his fortunes. Only the timely intervention of an old aunt had made Jessamy's season possible. Now, here she was again, entering Almack's on the arm of her late husband's cousin, a wealthy heiress in her own right, but with a quite different Earl of Wemyess. It smacked of irony.

Catching a glimpse of herself in one of the long mirrors in the hall, Jessamy thought that she had dressed rather scandalously for the occasion, but she was determined to wring a comment from Rand. The scooped bodice of her magenta gown was even lower than usual, and she wore no foile slip beneath the skirts. The gown, Mme. DuPont had insisted, was intended to show off her womanly curves. At least she had not wet the skirts as some women were known to do, to make them cling provocatively to their legs. It was a common thing, yet Jessamy refused to take such measures even to catch Rand Montgomery's attention!

Fastening a delicate, glittering chain of diamonds around her slender neck, Jessamy stood back from the mirror. Perfect. And she was certain Rand Montgomery would agree.

When Rand arrived promptly at a quarter till seven, she was satisfied to see the gleam of admiration in his eyes. If he thought she looked nice with a spangled shawl concealing her curves, Jessamy reflected with a feline smile, then he would most certainly think so when she removed it. And when they reached Almack's and Jessamy gave her shawl into the keeping of a servant, she was gratified to see Rand's sudden recoil, and the widening of his eyes to darkly shining orbs before they narrowed in grim consideration.

"Do you like my new gown, my lord?" she asked sweetly, and his gaze swept over her figure with deliberation, as if he had just noticed.

"Yes," he finally answered truthfully, "you are very beautiful, Jessamy. You are the most beautiful woman I have ever seen . . ."

She had not expected that compliment, and Jessamy's eyes widened. It was quite obvious he meant the comment, that he was not speaking in a mocking tone or idly, and she was at a loss for words.

"Thank you, my lord," she murmured finally, and he smiled.

"You are very welcome, my lady." He bent his arm

toward her. "Shall we enter? All eyes seem to be upon us now."

Her lips quirked in a teasing smile. "It must be because of your elegant burgundy coat and exquisite neck-cloth. As usual, you will have all of London buzzing before the night is over."

Laughing, Rand gazed at her so warmly that she found herself blushing like a schoolgirl. "*Au contraire*, madame! It is you who will have all of London buzzing," he disagreed. "And you already have me buzzing . . ."

Without another word he led her onto the dance floor, where they executed the steps of the cotillion in perfect rhythm. Rand was fully aware that most of the men in Almack's were staring at Jessamy, and when the set was over he led her to the refreshment table, a possessive hand upon her arm.

"No, thank you," she said when he asked if she would care for some of the small cakes or punch, "I'm afraid I cannot stomach the refreshments at Almack's. The cakes are always stale, and the punch insipid."

Rand's eyes twinkled as he teased, "And I thought you would never turn down food, my dear. What a surprise!"

"I'm full of surprises," she returned archly, lifting one shoulder as she regarded him with a smile. "And the evening has only begun, my lord."

Narrowing his eyes, Rand gazed back at her, doubt beginning to show in his expression. "I do hope that you recall why I asked you to be my escort this evening. I need for you to stay by my side, as . . ."

"As a barrier against all these simpering young females storming your formidable bastions, my lord?" Jessamy finished for him, then added innocently, "Or have we missed them this evening?'' she blinked her eyes in pretty confusion and glanced around the room.

Shaking his head, Rand said, "From the looks we're receiving, I should say that I will be needed as a barrier against all your admirers instead, my fair lady.'' He indicated a gentleman striding toward them with purposeful steps. "Lord Worthington approaches with a gleam in his eye that I have seen directed toward many a fair maiden in this city, so beware. He has a reputation for being the most deadly rake with the ladies, and has a well-earned name in the gaming hells as well.''

Jessamy flicked a wary glance toward Worthington, well aware of his identity, and recalled what she had heard also. Handsome, dissolute, well-heeled, and with absolutely no regard for the reputations of the young ladies he chose to honor with his attention, Lord William Richard Joseph Worthington, Duke of Lichfield, did exactly as he pleased.

At this moment, he was pleased to make himself known to Jessamy.

"How d'you do?'' he murmured suavely to Rand, but his eyes were centered upon the lovely lady by his side.

"Very well, thank you,'' Rand replied politely. "What brings you to this affair, Worthington? I had not thought you the man for Almack's.''

Worthington's full, sensual mouth curved into a smile, and his heavy eyes focused upon Rand for a moment. "Did you not? While it is true that I prefer tossing St. Hugh's bones, or a lively game of hazard, I am sometimes persuaded that I must seek more gentle entertainment in a more refined establishment than White's or Boodle's. What brings *you* here?''

"Dare I admit to the same inclination?'' Rand returned lightly. "Almack's is noted for its . . . gentle entertainment, as proven by the presence of the lovely lady at my side. May I introduce Lady Jessamy Montgomery to you?"

Worthington immediately bowed over the hand Jessamy held out to him, his eyes gleaming with appreciation.

"How d'you do, madam? I have, of course, heard of you before. You have not joined in society for some time."

"I have heard of you also, my lord," Jessamy replied so sweetly that the duke's eyes narrowed. "Who has not?" she added.

Nonplussed, the Duke of Lichfield gazed at Jessamy's wide eyes and bland expression, not at all convinced she was as innocent as she sounded. Nor was she at all the naîve young girl he'd first thought, but a woman in the first bloom of maturity, lovely and poised and fascinating.

Lord Worthington smiled and released her hand. "Indeed, who has not heard of me?" he returned lightly. "And who has not heard of—but seldom seen—the lovely Lady Montgomery who has whiled away these many years alone in a rambling house with an old man? I had often thought you must be myth instead of fact, but I can see I was mistaken."

"Yes, you were," Rand cut in smoothly, irritated beyond measure by Worthington's effrontery. "Lady Montgomery is very much fact, and very much in demand at the moment..." A lifted brow and pointed glance should have been enough to show Worthington the error of his ways, but alas, the gentleman seemed not to notice.

"I'm certain you won't mind surrendering the lady for a dance, Montgomery, old chap," Worthington was saying, taking Jessamy's hand and deftly leading her onto the dance floor. "It's been so deadly dull until your arrival with your lovely cousin..."

"Only if Lord Montgomery does not mind," Jessamy put in quickly, but Rand shrugged and shook his head.

"If the lady desires to dance, I will not stand in her way," Rand said stiffly. He stared after the couple as they swung onto the dance floor, then ground his teeth as the strains of a waltz filled the air. A waltz! And Worthington holding Jessamy much too closely!

Jessamy, stricken at Rand's apparent indifference, was also concerned with Worthington's attempts to hold her much too improperly. Propriety demanded more space between them, which she informed him curtly.

"I don't care to take chances with my reputation," she said, "especially at Almack's."

"Don't you ever take chances, my lady?" he asked. "A game of chance can be most exciting."

"I dare say." Jessamy concentrated for a moment on the steps of the waltz, holding Worthington at arm's length. He was entirely too distracting, with his hot eyes and bold words, and she wished she had stayed with Rand. Why had she bothered to attempt making him jealous when it was obvious he didn't care?

"Yes," Worthington was saying smoothly, "I have always been partial to games of chance, I suppose, in love as well as luck. But after all, aren't they much the same?"

"Not always. Dukes and earls are similar, yet I have found that they are not always the same," Jessamy replied.

Worthington smiled. "Touché, my lady." His hand pressed against the small of her back, swinging her in a graceful turn. "I have heard that Montgomery takes the most reckless chances in faro and wins; are you at all like your cousin?"

"And how do you mean that, may I ask, sir?" Jessamy demanded, beginning to dislike the duke quite heartily. He was wearing on her nerves, especially when she could see that Rand was paying rapt attention to a feather-headed young lady across the room, smiling down at her as she simpered—yes, simpered—and he had claimed to detest that affectation!

Worthington followed her glance, and his eyes narrowed with speculation. He swung her around once more, so that it was impossible for Jessamy to gaze at Rand, and said, "I mean that I will be most happy to place a wager with you on any of a number of objects, my lady. Just for amusement's sake, of course."

"Of course," Jessamy replied, distracted almost to fidgets. "I don't play cards well," she said absently, trying to pierce a screen of potted palm fronds to view Rand. "I never learned . . ."

"Then suggest a game. I play them all." Worthington swung her around again, and this time Jessamy could easily view the lovely young creature flanked by palm fronds and flaunting her charms at the earl. Rand was laughing heartily and enjoying himself entirely too much.

"A game?" Jessamy said, jerking her attention back to the duke, furious at Rand Montgomery. "Oh, yes—chess. I enjoy chess."

"Do you? How smashing! I am quite fond of the game myself. Shall we adjourn to the card room?" He was steering her toward an adjoining room before Jessamy could voice a protest.

"Wait!" She hung back, disengaging her arm from his grip. "I don't know if I should, my lord . . ."

"Do you suppose I have wicked intentions?" the duke asked, lifing one brow. "Don't be ridiculous! Not at Almack's, my dear. I would not risk being refused a voucher by Lady Jersey or Lady Cowper if I disgrace myself. It is quite safe,

I assure you. And to prove it, we will leave the doors open.''

Jessamy felt she could hardly refuse without appearing a pudding-heart, and as the duke was gazing at her so knowingly—had she been that transparent?—she felt the need to disguise her reaction to Rand as well.

"Very well," she said coolly. "Let us have a game of chess, my lord. And what are the stakes, since you insist upon a wager?"

"Ah, whatever my heart desires," he replied with a wicked leer that did his credit no good at all.

"Nonsense. I would never be such a gudgeon as to agree to those terms, my lord, and you must know that. Be reasonable," she stated firmly, seating herself in the wingback chair he drew back from the chess table. Candlelight glittered in her pale blond hair and it gleamed in soft shades of gold, framing Jessamy's heart-shaped face in loose curls that shifted with every movement. Wide blue eyes framed by sooty lashes regarded the duke with such intelligence and graveness that he experienced a momentary wave of doubt in his abilities, then scoffed at the idea.

"But my dear lady," he replied with a laugh, "that *was* reasonable! Since you object to such unlimited terms, however, may I suggest that if I win—which I am certain to do—you will bestow upon me a kiss..."

"Hardly better, Worthington!" Jessamy exclaimed indignantly. "Fie on you!" She gathered her shirts and half rose from the chair, but he put out a hand to detain her.

"Stay, please," he said. "What is a kiss, after all? And I will promise whatever you like, my lady."

Though about to refuse out of hand, Jessamy was struck with a sudden notion that appealed to her, and sank slowly back into her chair. A small smile tugged at the corners of

140

her mouth, those lips that the duke was even now gazing at so longingly, and she nodded.

"Very well. I have an excellent proposition for you, my lord. If I win—and may I say, that is quite possible—you must give your word to wed one of the poor ladies you have compromised so blithely with your wicked ways. A wife would give you some direction in life, I should think." Triumph glittered in her innocent blue eyes as she gazed sweetly at the duke's shocked countenance. "Oh? Perhaps you did not mean your rash promise to wager anything I liked?"

"No," he said hoarsely, and his voice cracked the tiniest bit. "No, I meant it. Of course I shall keep my word, as a Worthington always keeps his word. I do possess some sense of honor, you know."

"No, I didn't know. Excellent. Shall we begin the game, my lord? Black or white?" Jessamy settled herself in the chair and leaned her arms against the table, gazing down at the board of silver inlaid squares with massive playing pieces of silver and gold.

"Black."

"How appropriate. Then I shall move first, I believe."

Lord Worthington, Duke of Lichfield, nodded slowly, wondering if somehow he had been duped.

A small crowd had gathered round the table by the time the game was ended, yet it was a silent group, with only a few whispered comments and giggles here and there. The black scowls on the faces of the Duke of Lichfield and the Earl of Wemyess were puzzling mysteries that none present could solve, but the game had been a good one, with skill and tactical knowledge apparent in both opponents.

"Thank you for an excellent game, my lord," Jessamy

said, rising from her chair. She noted that Lichfield was a shade slower about rising to his feet than he had been earlier. "I hope you do not feel too disappointed that I have won?" she added kindly.

"What? Oh. No, no; smashing game, my lady, smashing." Worthington shook his head dazedly. "I simply don't know how . . . I've never lost . . . where did you learn that gambit, Lady Montgomery? I've never seen it before."

"From an old master, my lord." She smiled. "Now, it is late, and I . . ."

"Please . . . a boon . . . since the wager was a bit—uneven shall we say?—could I at least have the comfort of a consolation prize, perhaps?" he asked, and since he seemed so shaken at having lost, Jessamy nodded.

"That sounds fair, my lord. But nothing more than the original wager," she warned.

"That will be quite suitable," the duke agreed, still seeming rather stunned by his loss.

Jessamy was well aware of Rand's eyes on her as she threaded her way through the crowd, fielding queries from her acquaintances, as to the wager.

"What did you wager?" Melinda Fielding asked in a loud whisper, but Jessamy refused to answer.

She could feel Rand's eyes burning into her, and knew she would have to answer his questions later. She was in for a thundering scold.

✳ Chapter 15 ✳

Jessamy spent two days of blissful ignorance before fate overtook her in a cruel manner. Dressed in a simple frock of sprigged muslin, she had just completed her breakfast and was contemplating whether to answer her duty letters to relatives or enjoy an hour of sunshine in the garden, when Charles informed her that a gentleman awaited her pleasure in the drawing room.

"A gentleman, Charles? Not the earl?" Puzzled, Jessamy asked as to his identity and was informed that it was none other than the redoubtable rake, Lord Worthington. "My heavens!" she gasped. "Here? How very strange. I will be down in a moment, Charles. Do see to him."

"Certainly, my lady." Charles bowed himself out of her sitting room, closing the door with a slight click.

"Oh bother!" Lady Jessamy moaned, wringing her hands and sparing the hope that Rand would not choose to arrive while the duke was visiting. It would be quite awkward, especially in light of the sarcastic, scathing comments he had made to her after the chess game at Almack's.

"I do not understand how a supposedly intelligent woman can make such a cake of herself," he had said coldly, fixing her with a baleful eye. "You have a way of trying a man's patience, Lady Jessamy," he'd added.

She had answered all his set-downs meekly, biting her tongue to keep from replying in kind. There was no use in fueling the fires of his rage, and once he calmed down, Rand should be more amenable. Only now Worthington waited in the drawing room, and Rand was due to call upon her in a scant hour! She must get rid of the duke quickly.

"If the Earl of Wemyess calls before I am through with my interview with Lichfield, do put him in the small parlor," she informed Charles before entering the drawing room, and he nodded.

"Certainly, my lady"

Smoothing back the wisps of ruffled hair from her temples, Jessamy stepped into the drawing room with a determined smile.

"Good morning, Lord Worthington," she said. "I see that you are enjoying excellent health."

Smiling, Worthington stepped forward to take both her hands in his. "I am indeed, and feeling better by the moment as I gaze at your lovely face," he answered.

Jessamy heard the drawing-room doors click shut behind her. "Don't make me blush," she warned absently, listening to the faint noises in the entrance hall.

"I would like to make you blush," Worthington advised her, bringing Jessamy closer by the pressure of his hands.

Jessamy immediately recoiled, fixing him with a stern stare. "I do not appreciate your advances, sir," she rebuked the duke, but it had little effect. "I am not likely to succumb to your charms."

"But I have succumbed to your considerable charms, my lady..."

"Rubbish! You appreciate only the chase, my lord, and have no interest in the prize once it is obtained. That is why I wagered with you. I thought a proper set-down should do you some good, and marriage will settle you down even more."

"Ah, the wager!" Worthington said. "Yes, and that is why I am here, Lady Montgomery. I did lose our little wager, but if you recall, I was granted a consolation prize."

"The wager stipulated that you must wed this season," Jessamy reminded.

"I remember. But I set no limits upon *my* prize. I have come to claim my kiss."

Jessamy sighed. There was no avoiding it. She would have to honor her word or release Worthington from his, and that would never do. It had been a stroke of genius to suggest that he wed one of the poor ladies whom he had managed to compromise during the years, and she felt not a single twinge of pity for the man. He was a confirmed rake who deserved his sentence, though she was not at all certain that the poor wronged woman he would choose deserved her fate.

"Have you a wife in mind?" Jessamy asked promptly.

"As a matter of fact, I do," Lichfield replied. "But first—my consolation prize. Then you will hear all about the fortunate woman I have chosen to share the rest of my life."

Dutifully, Jessamy put up her face, expecting a brief brushing of the duke's lips across her mouth. After all, he could compromise her as easily as he had done the others if she was not careful.

But the Duke of Lichfield had different notions of a

proper kiss. He pulled her to him, taking her by surprise, and pressed his mouth over hers in a passionate embrace. Jessamy's hands were trapped between their bodies, and she struggled weakly against him. Worthington might have kissed her even more thoroughly, but a harsh voice behind them made him draw back in surprise.

"What the deuce is going on here?" Rand Montgomery demanded furiously.

Leaping backwards, Jessamy caught a glimpse of Rand's stormy face, and quailed. Doom. He would never understand.

"My lord," she began, but he flicked her an impatient glance and spoke directly to Worthington.

"Step outside with me," Rand commanded tersely, ignoring the fact that the duke outranked him.

"Certainly, since you asked so politely," Worthington mocked, winking at Jessamy, who glared at him as if he had three heads.

Whatever was Rand doing here almost an hour early? And why had Charles not put him in the small parlor as she had instructed? Squaring her shoulders, Jessamy lifted her chin as she set about undoing the considerable damage just done by Worthington.

"My dear Lord Montgomery," she began, but he cut her off quite shortly.

"I believe you should retire to your rooms for a time," Rand said. "I will take the liberty of . . . entertaining your guest."

Gaping at him, Jessamy opened her mouth to state quite emphatically that she most certainly would *not* be sent to her room as if she were an errant child, then noted the steely glint in Rand's eyes. His expression brooked no refusal, and she yielded the point.

"How kind of you!" she said tartly, a parting shot, then

turned to Lord Worthington, who was watching the proceedings with an amused twist to his mouth. No doubt, he had experienced this sort of occurrence quite often in his checkered career as a profligate. "Good day, Lord Worthington," she said, and turned to leave the room with her head held high.

The two men watched Jessamy sail from the drawing room, her skirts swishing across the elegant Turkish carpet, then turned to gaze warily at one another.

"Shall we?" Rand asked pleasantly, indicating with a sweep of one arm the same doors that had just seen Jessamy's departure.

"Of course," Worthington returned smoothly. "I assume you no longer wish to remain here? Am I to duel with you, my lord, because if I am, I must inform you that I am known to be an excellent swordsman and an even better shot."

"Really?" Rand's mouth curled in amusement. "How interesting, my lord. Why don't we take a turn in my curricle while we discuss the matter more fully."

Shrugging his expensively garbed shoulders, Worthington suffered himself to be led to Rand's carriage, giving his own smart turn-out directions to wait.

"Fine horses," Rand remarked coolly, gazing at the highstepping grays Worthington had purchased from Tattersall's'.

"Yes," the duke acknowledged, "they are."

The curricle rolled away from the curb and down the street, and Rand launched into a discussion immediately. He drove his own rig, so the two men had complete privacy.

"It seems that you admire my little cousin," he said to the duke, "but I am not at all certain that she needs your attention."

"I find her very intelligent and quite beautiful," Worthington admitted promptly. "Do you mind if I smoke?"

"Not at all," Rand returned politely. "I won't have you using Lady Jessamy, Worthington. She has been through too many trials in her life to endure the ruining of her reputation by a man such as you."

"That could be considered a grave insult, my lord," the duke returned mildly. "And don't be ridiculous—we only kissed."

"Enough to ruin a woman in London, you know that," Rand said tartly. "How many other women have you 'only' kissed, Worthington, but who are pariahs on the fringe of society today because of your attentions? Too damned many, as I have heard it! I won't have Jessamy included in that number."

"You would withdraw your suit because of a kiss?" the duke asked lightly, observing Montgomery's reaction with malicious glee.

"My suit?"

"Yes, of course, old man. You don't suppose for a moment that I believe you are doing this out of family obligation, do you? Don't try and gammon me with such flummery, because I am an old hand at this, Montgomery."

"What was the wager with Jessamy?" Rand demanded instead of attempting to answer Worthington's charge.

"The wager? Ah, that's the rub, is it?" Worthington shrugged carelessly. "Simple enough, old man. I wagered her a kiss against my marriage . . ."

"I beg your pardon!"

"It does sound a bit extreme, I know, but as I have only recently been informed by my grandmother—who holds the purse strings to the family fortune—that my funds will be cut off if I do not comport myself decently and wed some

148

fortunate young lady, I thought Lady Montgomery's wager quite amusing. And as I had not a thing to lose, it was extremely entertaining. Alas, I had not expected her to be such an excellent chess player," he added sadly.

"So you are to marry," Rand mused, slightly relieved. "Who is the girl?"

Worthington's heavy-lidded eyes glittered. "Your cousin should suffice. I have not found a woman in some time who has spirit, intelligence, and beauty, and I admit to being intrigued by her. And before you refuse out of hand," he said quickly, seeing from Rand's tensed shoulders and fierce expression that he was about to explode, "let me remind you that my family is quite powerful and wealthy. She could hardly do better in that respect, though I am the black sheep. Would you rob your lovely cousin of all that I could offer?"

Deep grooves bracketed Rand's mouth as he considered Worthington's shocking proposal. Could *he* offer Jessamy more? And he would never be happy in England, and did not know if she would thrive in America. Perhaps it would be the best thing for Jessamy . . .

"I do have *some* principles," Worthington was saying, "and once I wed I intend to be as good a husband to my bride as I can be—which is," he added wryly, "one reason I have not wed yet. I did not relish the notion of confining my talents to one woman."

The curricle took a corner, and Rand pulled on the ribbons so harshly that his matched grays jerked to a halt. A muscle twitched in his jaw as he regarded Worthington with dislike, but his voice was cool and colorless.

"The decision rests with Jessamy, but if she should accept your proposal, I will expect you to be faithful and never cause her any pain. Do we understand one another, Worthington?''

"Are you threatening me, my lord?" Worthington asked, lifting one brow.

"Most definitely."

The duke smiled. "How quaint. Yes, I understand you quite well." He stepped from the curricle to the curb and stood for a moment looking up at Rand. "We are very much alike in some ways, Montgomery. It's a pity we have to be on opposite sides of the fence, what?"

Rand leveled a glance at the duke and shrugged. "Just be certain you give Lady Jessamy no cause for complaint, for it would distress me greatly."

Slapping the ribbons against his horses' gleaming rumps, Rand deftly guided the curricle away from the curb and Lord Worthington.

Jessamy was more than a little wary when Lord Worthington was announced again, and descended the sweep of stairs with trepidation. Her eyes betrayed no signs of the few tears she had shed, but her mouth was clamped in a firm line as she approached the duke.

"To what do I owe this dubious pleasure?" she asked shortly. "Another attempt at scandal, my lord?"

Worthington had the grace to look ashamed, and swept one arm toward the small parlor. "Shall we discuss this in private, my lady?"

"Not for an instant! I refuse to allow you the liberty of so much as a moment in which to tarnish my reputation, my lord!"

"Then it shall be discussed here in the entrance hall in full view of the servants. I am certain the tale will be repeated over and over again in all the great houses of London. You surely realize how servants talk."

Surrendering to the truth, Jessamy allowed Worthington his moment of privacy just inside the open doors of the parlor, her arms crossed over her chest and her chin firmly thrust out. "What is it you wish to speak to me about?"

"Only this, my lady—I have chosen my bride."

Surprised, Jessamy thawed slightly. "You have? But that is excellent news, Worthington! I find it amazing that you will honor our wager . . . "

"But I am an honorable man in most respects," the duke argued. "It is only my well-earned reputation as a rake that has blackened my family name. As you must realize, the Worthingtons are of excellent lineage, and great importance in England."

"I know that. It was never your family's fault that you tarnished the name. Who is the blushing bride, my lord? I do hope you chose a woman you had compromised, as the wager stipulated."

"I most certainly have," the duke said promptly, and he took one of Jessamy's hands, being careful to remain a respectful distance.

A feeling of disquiet pricked Jessamy, and she gazed at Worthington warily, listening first with astonishment, then dismay as he explained how he had chosen her to be his bride, and how her cousin had already agreed to the match.

"I would care for you and your daughter most diligently," the duke promised earnestly, unaware that Jessamy's stony silence was due to horrified shock.

Her face registered little of her suffering as Jessamy realized with a sense of bitterness that Rand must care very little for her at all. And to think she had begun to feel as if he cared! What a fool she was! He had only come with them to England in order to ensure that she find a husband, thus relieving himself of any obligation. Kenilworth had never been a consideration, and Chastity, dear sweet Chastity, would suffer also at this final betrayal. Bright tears stung her eyes, and she blinked them back.

"Lady Jessamy?" Worthington was saying, and she realized with a start that he was staring at her oddly.

"Oh! pardon me! I was thinking . . . "

"But not about my proposal, I warrant," Worthington guessed shrewdly. "I imagine you were thinking of Montgomery. Oh, don't deny it. I've seen your eyes when you look at him, though I think you rather foolish to reject me for a man who is too cocklebrained to speak out for you."

Jessamy colored hotly. "But I never said . . . "

Worthington waved a weary hand. "You don't have to say it, my lovely goosecap. It's as plain as the charming little nose on your face—you are mad about Montgomery." He shrugged. "A lamentable position, but there you have it. What do you intend to do?"

"What . . . what can I do?" Jessamy found herself asking, and marveled at how quickly the situation had changed. "He does not say a word about how he feels."

"Trust me." Worthington said, and oddly enough she believed him. "I have a method for drawing out our quarry that is bound to work."

Jessamy half smiled. How desperate she had become in her love for Rand.

✳ Chapter 16 ✳

If Worthington had made his plans clear to Jessamy, she would have refused cooperation immediately. No one possessing their right faculties would ever countenance such a ridiculous, dangerous thing as a *duel* just to gain the attention of another party. That was doing it way too brown.

But as it was, Jessamy left for Kenilworth without ever knowing that while she was tucked safely inside her landau rocking along the roads from London, Worthington was preparing himself for a duel, with a satisfied smile, to boot. He had carefully concocted this scheme and was quite proud of himself indeed. If Rand Montgomery wanted Lady Jessamy as wife, then he would have to fight for her. It had been done since feudal times—no, since cavemen roamed England— and he saw no good reason why it shouldn't be done now.

Of course, he wanted her also, but Lady Jessamy would never agree as long as her heart yearned for the Earl of Wemyess. The matter had to be settled to the satisfaction of one and all.

First on Worthington's agenda was his refreshing note to

Rand requesting the honor of his presence in his annual box at the upcoming opera. The note was duly written and delivered to Montgomery's townhouse, whereupon Rand considered declining the invitation. He was quite certain that Jessamy would be a special guest of the duke's, and Rand had no desire to sit like a gudgeon and watch. But, after careful deliberation, the earl concluded that if Jessamy was to wed the duke, he must appear as though he thought it a worthy match. He did not, of course, but since he had given Worthington his blessing in a fit of pique, he was bound to his word. Now Rand was consumed with chagrin at the thought of Jessamy wedding the duke. And why not, when he was in love with her himself?

Love, however, was not the issue. Clearly, Jessamy had faced considerable difficulty adjusting to life at Idlewood, and she still had the notion that Kenilworth must belong to Chastity. Since Idlewood was Rand's home and the only place he truly wished to reside, how could he ask Jessamy to leave the home she loved, to stay with him? He couldn't. He wouldn't. Worthington, however, could. The reprehensible duke had much to offer Jessamy in the way of wealth and position, and perhaps he would reform once wed. Stranger things had happened, though Rand doubted the duke's ability to conform. One large concern was the child. He had grown quite fond of Chastity, and wanted to see her happy. A match between Worthington and Lady Jessamy would assure Chastity's place in English society. And he could bestow Kenilworth upon her just as her mother wished . . .

So Rand decided to attend the opera. He could endure much for the comfort of knowing that he was doing it for Jessamy and Chastity, he decided later, suffering his valet's attempts to tie a perfect cravat.

"But it is called a waterfall, my lord," the valet moaned, "and I cannot seem to manage it! I should have been a footman, or a groom, or..."

"Enough of your self-chastisement," Rand interrupted wearily, reaching up to tie his cravat with quick, efficient motions that left the English valet open-mouthed. "I learned this knot some time ago, so do not fret yourself, man."

As he bowed to a superior wisdom, the valet's estimation of this rough American rose several notches. He may have been born in the colonial atmosphere of mediocrity, but Rand Montgomery certainly had the breeding and background to rival any native Englishman's!

And garbed in the long, flowing opera cloak that gentlemen of the day were wearing, he appeared every inch the aristocrat. He wore a silk top hat and carried a silver-headed cane, and the valet gave an appreciative sigh as Rand left the house. He was worthy of his valet's talents.

It was a crisp summer night. Stars lit the sky like a million tiny diamonds, sparkling so brightly they rivaled the moon. The opera house was already teeming when Rand arrived, its lanterns and lamps glowing so brilliantly that they drowned out the moon and stars overhead.

Rand gave his equipage into the care of his tiger and entered the opera house, secure in the knowledge that he had resigned himself to Jessamy's affection for the Duke of Lichfield. Jewels glittered and sparkled, and the patent leather shoes that the men wore gleamed like polished glass as they moved around the carpeted floor. Rand scanned the crowd for a moment, tempted to yield to the English affectation and put up his quizzing glass to view the throng as he had seen so many men do.

His spirits lifted briefly when he spotted Worthington by a

huge pedestal bearing a potted palm, but he did not spy Jessamy.

"Worthington," Rand acknowledged the duke's hail as he turned. "How are you this evening?"

"This is a most elegant affair, Montgomery," the duke said with a laugh. "Wouldn't you say?"

"It's better than Almack's," Rand conceded. "At least the company here is out for more than catching a wealthy husband, and every young thing garbed in pink and white does not try to snag you as you pass."

"So cynical already?" Worthington mocked. "You amaze me, Montgomery. I would have thought you'd be flattered by all the attention."

"How strange. That's exactly what Lady Jessamy said," Rand observed. "And speaking of Lady Jessamy..."

"Were we?"

"Yes. Where is she tonight?"

"And how should I know that, my dear chap?" Worthington lifted his quizzing glass on its black satin ribbon to peer at Rand as if he were an insect beneath a glass.

Rand's eyes narrowed. "Perhaps I misunderstood. I was under the impression that you would know the lady's location."

"How quaint—but wrong."

"Is there a reason why you should not know where she is?" Rand asked with decreasing patience.

"There certainly is, old boy! Haven't you heard the latest on-dit?" Worthington tilted his head and gazed at Rand with surprise.

"What the devil are you talking about? Heard what?" Rand demanded in a growl.

"Why, the simple fact that I am no longer interested in the lady. It's as simple as that, old chap." Worthington waved a languid hand in the direction of a beautiful young woman who stood several feet away. She was smiling at him, and Rand sensed that there was an intimacy between them that had more to it than simple friendship. "If you will note that young lovely," Worthington pointed out in a lazy drawl, "you will see my new *amour*. Isn't she a delightful young thing? Skin like alabaster, eyes like stars, and . . ."

"Have you run mad?" Rand demanded.

"Mad? I? My dear boy, what a silly thing to ask!" the duke said. "But in a way, I suppose I am mad—mad with passion for the young lady we see now. Since I met her I have thought of little else."

"And Lady Jessamy?" Rand's hands had curled into fists at his side, but he controlled himself with an effort.

"Ahh, Lady Jessamy." Worthington shook his head sadly. "The spoils of love are ofttimes like the spoils of war," he began in a poetic tone.

"Rubbish!" Rand said rudely. "I cannot believe that you are serious, Worthington, and not jesting."

"I never jest in matters of love, dear boy. It's simply not done, nor is it my style. Your lovely Lady Jessamy is . . . well . . ." Leaning forward, he whispered in a low tone, "Why buy the cow when the milk is free?"

Rage flooded Rand in a consuming tide. "What did you say?" he muttered through clenched teeth.

"I was explaining to you my reasons, Montgomery. Really, you should pay more attention lest you be considered quite rude. Shall I put it bluntly?"

"Please do."

"I just do not feel the *need* to wed the lady anymore. And to be polite, I have thrown her over for another. I believe the dear girl returned to the country to recover from her broken heart."

"I should kill you!" Rand hissed, taking a step forward, his jaw tight and eyes blazing with fury.

The duke's quizzing glass lifted again, then dropped. "Now, Montgomery, aren't you taking this entire affair a bit too seriously?"

Aware of the curious onlookers, and the fact that Jessamy's name would be spattered with the mud of gossip, Rand said quietly, "I believe that you should realize the gravity of the situation, Worthington, before I find it necessary to land you a leveler right here."

"Here? At the opera house? How droll! I daresay, man, if you intend to be barbaric, this is not the time nor the place, what?"

"Barbaric? You *English* are so refined, courteous, and polite, I suppose! Perhaps I should speak from a script like one of the actors onstage?"

"Yes, perhaps you should," the duke agreed with a curious smile. "But aren't we civilized men?"

"One of us is!"

"Then, my civilized gentleman from America, suggest something civilized to do if you are so insulted!"

"One against one," Rand said softly, "Anytime, any place, any weapon you like."

The quizzing glass rose again. "A duel? You are suggesting a duel? What a ridiculous notion . . ."

"Do you prefer murder?"

"Ah, I see." Worthington was quiet for a moment. "Very well. Hyde Park, after midnight. I haven't seen this opera yet, and I've heard it's quite good. I should hate to miss the first act if we fight now, Montgomery."

Dueling was an old custom with the English. In America, it was just termed a fight most of the time, unless, of course, one went to all the trouble to name seconds, choose weapons, and call in a physician and even a priest.

As Rand's anger cooled, he began to wish he had just hit the duke instead of challenging him. Yet that would not have regained Jessamy's honor, nor destroyed the man who had so callously used her with no regard.

A bright moon hung in the sky when he reached the shadowy outskirts of the park, glittering along the paths and across the dew-wet grass. Rand paused, reining in his mount, searching in the night for lanterns that would mark the location of the duke.

He'd waited for only a few moments when he was approached by a lone gentleman in a short cape. "You are the Earl of Wemyess?" the man inquired.

"I am," was the short reply.

"Then please to follow me, sir." The young man paused, looking past Rand for a moment before he turned and asked, "Have you no second, sir?"

"No. I do not need one," Rand answered. "Lead on."

Though flustered, and muttering that it was not usual to conduct an affair of honor improperly, the young man led his horse to a secluded clearing in the park.

"Ah, Montgomery," a voice said loudly from a cluster of trees to the left. "Right on time, I see."

"Did you doubt it? I am a man who keeps his promises," Rand said, dismounting from his horse. He paused, coolly peeling off his leather gloves as his eyes adjusted to the dim light provided by moon and lanterns.

"I was challenged, so I choose the weapons," the duke said as if Rand were totally ignorant of the correct procedure for a duel.

"And the weapon you choose?" Rand asked carelessly, removing his cloak.

There was something in the American's tone that gave the Duke of Lichfield pause, and he stared through the gloom at Rand. Perhaps this had not been such a good idea after all, Worthington mused before Rand's mocking repetition of his earlier query pierced his thoughts.

"I said, what weapons do we use, Worthington?"

"Rapiers." Worthington smiled. "I find them so much more civilized than pistols. Have you ever fenced, my lord?"

"No. I've never considered weapons toys, Your Grace." Rand's bland smile never wavered as the duke drew in his breath sharply at the implied rebuke. "In America, we have little time for such sport. But I am certain, I shall have no difficulty."

"Very well," the duke snapped. He'd not considered the fact that Montgomery might refuse to admit his lack of proficiency with rapiers, and had hoped for a draw instead of an actual duel. It was apparent that the earl would not back down.

Worthington's second held out a black lacquered case and snapped it open so that the opponents could select their weapons. A pair of thin rapiers reposed on a bed of maroon velvet, gleaming lethally wicked in the moonlight.

"You choose," the duke said shortly, and Rand shrugged.

He reached in and lifted one of the thin-bladed swords, testing it in the palm of one hand for balance, and the duke was relieved to see that apparently the American did know something of swords.

"Shall we?" Worthington said politely, indicating the direction of the clearing with a wave of one hand.

"Of course."

Both men removed their coats and took their places facing one another, legs bent slightly at the knees, swords held in front of them with one edge almost touching the tips of their noses.

"*En garde!*" came the command, and the rapiers tilted forward while the opponents' left arms lifted to the rear. Only the right sides of their bodies were exposed to the thrust of the blades, and the small semicircle of watchers held their breaths as it became apparent that this was not merely a play of swords, but deadly earnest.

Lunge, parry, riposte, thrust, feint—the movements of both men were quick and agile, and each realized the other's proficiency as the gleaming Toledo steel clanged again and again, ringing in the still of the night as loud as church bells. Sweat poured down their faces, dripping onto the shirts they wore, drenching them so that the cloth stuck to their bodies. Lamplight wavered in nervous pools as the duke's second held his lamp high, and the clearing was quiet but for the clashing of the blades and heavy breathing of the opponents.

Once Worthington almost slipped upon the wet grass, and another time the duke's thrust caught Rand off balance. Rand fell to one knee on the grass, and the Duke of Lichfield plunged his blade forward, slicing into Rand's thigh with a quick, clean motion. Worthington pulled back immediately, a faint smile on his mouth as he began to ask if Rand wished to forfeit the match.

"Hell no!" the American earl growled, leaping to his feet with an efort. His pain-contorted face gave the lie to his insistence that he was unharmed, and only when the physician reluctantly gave his approval did the duel begin again.

This time Rand's slashing attack was so fierce that it caught Worthington by surprise, driving him back. The duke failed to parry a forward lunge, and Rand's blade drove in under his guard to pierce his side. Worthington fell back, his rapier dropping to the ground as his second rushed forward.

"Enough!" the young man cried, face pale as he looked up from the duke's prostrate form. "I believe he may be mortally wounded."

The physician pushed him away roughly, and the young man rose to face Rand, who returned his hot gaze calmly. "I regret the foolishness that prompted this, but I was given little choice," Rand said.

"Leave! Quickly, before the King's soldiers get wind of it and arrive," the young man said bitterly. "It will be all over London soon enough."

Shrugging, Rand thrust the duke's rapier into the ground at his feet, gave the duke one last glance, then pivoted and limped to his waiting horse. Blood was seeping from his wound, and he had to seek assistance.

As the hoofbeats faded in the dark, the duke's head rose from its grassy bed. He grimaced, snapping, "Get away from me, you leech! I can scarce breathe with you all crowding about me like mourners at a funeral!"

"Are you well, Your Grace?" the young man asked anxiously, returning to the duke's side.

"Of course, you young idiot! I'm not dead, and would not even have sustained this scratch if you had tied the vest on properly as I told you!"

"But I did!" was the protest. "You should not have received any injury!"

"Well, Montgomery's blade pierced this damnable piece of cowhide like it was butter, fool!" The Duke of Lichfield stumbled to his feet, regarding his torn shirt somberly. "It's a good thing I wore it, what? I might have been poked if I hadn't had the foresight to do so."

"You certainly gave a good show, Your Grace."

The duke looked pleased. "Didn't I? I once thought I might like to act upon the stage, but I was young then. Perhaps I should have trod the boards." He shrugged. "Ah well, at least Montgomery will have food for thought."

"You were marvelous, Your Grace!"

"Yes, yes! Now take me home before I bleed like a stuck pig!"

✳ Chapter 17 ✳

Jessamy rambled about the vast rooms and gardens of Kenilworth fretfully, wondering if Worthington's plan would work as he had promised. She had returned to Kenilworth the very next day; yet, two weeks had passed without a word from Rand Montgomery. Had he abandoned them? How could she put The Plan into order if Rand would not appear for her to do so? And just what was The Plan? Perhaps Worthington did not know what he was doing after all. Jessamy could not conceive in her wildest dreams what scheme the Duke of Lichfield had concocted on her behalf. She could only wonder if she had made some grave error in her judgment of the man.

Disillusionment had removed some of the luster from her previous determination, and now she was filled with all sorts of doubts. Even her cherished Kenilworth was beginning to appear foreign now. She felt as if she had no roots, as though Kenilworth was no longer home to her anymore. After all, the estate did belong to Rand now. Was she selfish to want Kenilworth for her daughter—Jamie's child? Nothing felt as it did before . . . before her trip to Baltimore.

Frustrated, Jessamy batted at long waving fronds of a lilac bush as she took tea in the garden. Conflicting emotions warred within her, yet she could do little but wait.

She was on her fourth cup of tea when she heard a small commotion echoing through the garden. It sounded like Chastity when she was excited. Jessamy decided to investigate the cause, and rose from the lounge chair, smoothing her skirts as she ambled in the direction of the noise.

Chastity was gamboling about like a puppy, laughing and clapping her hands at something Jessamy could not see. A faint smile curved her mouth at the child's carefree manner and melodic laughter. The smile was still on her lips when she stepped through the high hedge with its archway of greenery and saw the reason for Chastity's amusement.

Rand Montgomery was standing in the garden close to a profusion of pink tearoses, his handsome face creased in a smile as he gazed fondly at the golden-haired girl and the fat kitten he had brought her. A ball of fluff was prancing across the clipped lawn, pausing occasionally to tease Chastity's feet, then dart off in another direction.

"Oh look, Mummy!" Chastity cried, clapping her hands as she saw her mother standing in the garden, "Uncle Rand has brought me a kitten!"

"Yes, I see, darling," Jessamy murmured, her eyes devouring Rand's lean frame and handsome face. He was returning her gaze wearily. "Welcome to Kenilworth, Lord Montgomery," she said primly, dropping him a curtsy.

His wary gaze altered to a frown. "Good afternoon, *cousin*. I trust that you are in better spirits now that you are safely in *your* home . . ."

165

Nodding uneasily, Jessamy wondered at his tone, but did not argue. "I am quite contented," she managed to whisper.

"Then I am pleased you have renewed yourself," he said shortly. He gestured to the sprawling stone house covering the better part of two acres. "Shall we go up to the manor? I have yet to see it . . ."

"Of course, my lord," she said promptly, gesturing to a servant hovering nearby to see to his ladyship's needs. "I will have your baggage brought in and put in the west wing. Your father's room was there."

Rand who found it difficult to believe that his father had ever been reared in this house, inclined his head like visiting royalty, which irritated Jessamy to the hilt. Must he behave so coolly? It was true that she had provoked him, but he was doing the distant earl charade a bit too brown! Pivoting, Jessamy started toward the house with quick, short steps.

Her irritation must have been evident, for Rand's voice was a mixture of amusement and sarcasm when he asked if she would please repeat the directions to the west wing.

"I'm afraid I didn't quite understand your directions, Lady Jessamy."

Halting, she turned around. "Have you been hurt?" she interrupted, noting his limp as he walked behind her.

"You could say that," was the enigmatic answer. "Right now I am quite weary and in need of refreshment, so if you would please direct me to my room, or have one of your servants do so, I would be most grateful."

"Certainly," she said stiffly. "I will show you to your chambers myself."

Rand was silent on the walk through the vast, echoing halls of the stone manor house, gazing up at suits of armor and war weapons with just as much interest as he viewed the paintings of his ancestors.

"Very impressive," he observed at last as they trod the steps leading to the second floor. "I can almost hear the pomp and circumstance with which my ancestors lived."

"Oh no, you can't really imagine it," Jessamy replied with a smile. "I used to pore through the old account books just for entertainment, trying to piece together what it must have been like in the 1600s. It was quite different from today, I can tell you."

Rand had a sudden mental picture of a bored and lonely Jessamy sitting in an empty room with dusty ledgers and account books, and his heart gave a lurch. Was it any wonder she was being so reserved?

"Even back then," Jessamy was saying with a mischievous twinkle in her eyes, "one traveled with no less than ten or fifteen servants, so you can see that I did you an enormous favor by limiting the number I took to America."

Rand's mouth twitched. "Yes, I realize now what a sacrifice you must have made. I appreciate your thoughtfulness."

"Thank you, my lord. It's nice to be appreciated." She swung open the door to a small drawing room and stepped inside, leaving Rand to follow. Tufted chairs and settees of burgundy and gold lined the walls. Lacquered tables inlaid with gilt designs held ornate clocks and brass boxes. At the opposite end of the room stood the wide, high bed, draped with heavy material and looking as if it should belong to a king. Four posts upheld the draperies, and a small carved railing had been placed around it as if setting it apart.

"It's . . . elegant," Rand murmured, cocking one eyebrow dubiously. His glance said much more than his words, and Jessamy laughed.

"Do you like it better than your less ornate furnishings at Idlewood?" she teased.

Rand cleared his throat. "Well, no," he admitted, "but it is very nice. Does it have a bath?"

"I will have a servant bring you water so that you might wash away the road dust before dinner," Jessamy said. "Shall I give you directions to the dining hall?"

"Oh, no. I would prefer dining in my room tonight. But when I do decide to explore, I shall ask for directions from a servant." Rand regarded her with his dark eyes, gazing down at her through his lashes with such an enigmatic expression that Jessamy could not speak for a moment.

Finally gathering her thoughts, she offered, "I shall show you Kenilworth. No one else can do it justice. Though I am a Montgomery only by marriage, I have lived in this house for eight years. I know and love it as no one else does." She smiled. "It will be one of my greatest pleasures to show the estate to a true Montgomery, my lord."

Rand was silent, and his eyes flickered with troubled shadows. He lifted one hand as if he intended to touch her, then let his hand drop by his side and smiled. "I would be most pleased if you would do so, Lady Jessamy. I shall look forward to seeing Kenilworth through your eyes."

The morning sun filtered through the yards of damask curtaining the windows of the room that had seen generations of Montgomerys break their fast each morning. Jessamy sat at the head of the table as she had done for years, shuffling through the post and separating correspondence from business. An empty plate held the remains of what had been, as usual, a large meal.

"I see that your appetite hasn't diminished," Rand said as he entered the room. He pulled out a chair and sat down opposite her. "Too bad I cannot say the same for your reputation."

Choking on a sip of hot tea, Jessamy looked up, startled

and confused. "I beg your pardon," she managed to say. "Whatever are you talking about?"

Nodding to a hovering servant, Rand allowed his plate to be filled with kidney pie, smoked fish, scones, and a rasher of bacon. "May I please have coffee rather than tea?" he asked the man, who flashed a startled glance at him.

"Of course, my lord," the man replied smoothly, quickly recovering from his surprise. "I shall bring it at once."

"Randolph," Jessamy said to the servant, "I had Cook prepare some especially for his lordship."

Bowing, Randolph acknowledged this information with a flash of relief. Coffee was an unusual request, and he had not been at all certain there was so much as one coffee bean on the entire estate, yet as a well-trained servant, he was expected to comply with every request.

As soon as Randolph discreetly disappeared, Jessamy turned back to Rand, one delicate brow lifted inquiringly. "Please explain your last remark to me."

"I wasn't aware an explanation was needed, madam," Rand replied. "Is that strawberry jam in that silver urn?"

"Yes it is. Of course an explanation is needed."

Rand looked up at her from the toast he was spreading with a thick layer of jam. "I never discuss unpleasant matters while I eat."

Sitting back, Jessamy waited. He was, of course, toying with her. He would reveal soon enough what he had on his mind, and any attempts to draw him out would obviously be met with rebuffs.

It wasn't until they had completed a tour of the grounds and were on the third floor of the manor house that the subject was broached again. Rand had commented on the spacious rooms, and was completely awed by the High Great Chamber with its painted murals and gilt carvings.

"Jamie loved this room also, though I find it rather oppressive for some reason," Jessamy said. "You and Jamie seem to have a lot in common, but that is only natural, I suppose, as you were cousins."

"That is part of the reason I feel so responsible," Rand said heavily, moving to stand in front of a long case window. The sun slanted through the thick panes of leaded glass, making his face seem harsher in the strong light. He turned back to Jessamy. "I should never have countenanced your introduction to Worthington," he said roughly.

"And why is that, my lord?" Jessamy asked carefully, recalling the duke's strict orders to play upon Rand's more sensitive feelings. She was to appear vulnerable and hurt.

"Because the man is a bounder, a cad, and you were not protected by your family as you should have been."

"Yes. It has been . . . terrible," Jessamy sighed, letting her gaze drop to the floor and her shoulders droop. "I am not certain how I have managed."

"Damme, but I feel like an insufferable boor! And the duke refuses to retract . . ." He paused, his face darkening, and pivoted to stare out the window as he struggled for control.

Alarm began to fill Jessamy. Just what had Worthington said to Rand? Surely, the duke would do nothing *too* preposterous—would he?

She moved forward to lay a soft hand upon Rand's sleeve. "It's all right, my lord. Matters will smooth over," she comforted, wondering wildly what she was talking about. How could she ask without appearing the fool?

"Hmm-hmm," Jessamy cleared her throat. "I . . . I . . . cannot help but ask how you . . . discovered . . . this."

Whirling, Rand gazed at her for a moment, his face in harsh relief, light and shadow, his eyes piercing her with reproach. "Worthington told me," he said. "Now it only remains to decide how this delicate matter should be handled in the future. With your reputation in shreds, it will not be easy . . ."

"I beg your pardon?"

Rand stared at her. "I said, with your reputation in shreds, it will not be easy."

"That's what I thought you said," Jessamy replied harshly, damning Worthington for a fiend. "My lord, would it be asking too much for you to tell me just *how much* the duke told you? I know it's probably painful for you to relate, but I would be so grateful." Fury warred with common sense as Jessamy dampened the urge to explode into a temper tantrum such as she had not thrown since she was in leading strings.

"Why, he explained—at my insistence—how he had compromised you, then thrown you over for another. Of course, some of the details I refused even to consider repeating."

"That's quite all right," Jessamy said politely. "I am certain the duke was thorough." Wait until she saw Worthington again!

"He certainly was," Rand agreed. "Which is why I have decided to take Chastity back to America with me. It may take some time for all this to die down, and I know you would not want—"

"I beg your pardon?" Jessamy all but shouted. "You intend to take my child?"

Rand blinked. "But of course. You would not wish her to be uncomfortable or shunned in any way, so . . ."

Speaking between her teeth, Jessamy struggled for composure as she said, "Chastity will remain with me, as she always has. As for this farce, I cannot go on with it. I must explain . . ."

"No." Rand held up a hand. "I refuse to listen to any more explanations, Lady Jessamy. My patience has been stretched to the limit, and I am afraid of my reaction should I have to listen to any more explanations!"

"But—"

"No," he said adamantly. "I cannot risk losing control again, not that I would do to you what I did to Worthington . . ."

"What . . . did you do to Worthington?" Jessamy asked fearfully.

Rand faced her with a stony expression, his eyes hard. "I challenged him to a duel."

❋ Chapter 18 ❋

Shock rendered Jessamy speechless. Had Worthington planned that reaction from Rand? Surely not! He might be reckless, but the duke was hardly foolish!

By eight of the following morning she had already scrawled several furious missives to the Duke of Lichfield, who was, Rand had informed her, laid up in his bed recovering from a minor saber wound. Each letter had been crumpled up, however, and thrown upon her floor. Now she sat with her chin propped in one hand, gazing at her frowning reflection in the far mirror. She was in the soup for certain.

Sighing, Jessamy rose from her rosewood writing desk and left her chambers, wandering restlessly through the halls. She paused briefly in the schoolroom to listen to Chastity's lessons, then moved on.

She was loitering in the greenhouse when Melinda Fielding called, dressed in a bright yellow outfit that matched her new tilbury.

"See?" Melinda said with a laugh, turning so that Jessamy could admire both her gown and the two-wheeled vehicle with plush velvet cushions of yellow. "I am quite the thing, am I not?"

"That you are," Jessamy agreed fondly. "How did you know I needed your company, Melinda?"

"I didn't. Perhaps it was intuition that brought me here." Melinda joined her friend with a rustle of her skirts and the taffeta parasol she carried. "Shall we take tea in the garden instead of putter with plants, my dear? I had quite a time finding you, you know, and am not at all partial to grubbing in the dirt."

Laughing again, Jessamy tucked her hand through Melinda's arm. "I was just inspecting the growth of some new plants I brought back from America. Tea sounds wonderful."

They ambled along stone paths through the terraced gardens, pausing at last on the wide veranda where tea would be served.

"So tell me all about your fascinating cousin," Melinda begged prettily, tugging off her gloves. Soft dark hair framed her oval face in silky curls, and her cheeks were rosy. "Has he come to visit yet?"

Grateful for someone she could talk to, Jessamy confided, "Yes he has, Melinda, and oh! such a terrible thing has happened!"

"Merciful heaven! From the expression on your face, I can see that this is no jest, Jessamy! Whatever has happened?"

"Worthington!" Jessamy blurted. "Do you recall how I told you he had some sort of plan in mind that would bring Rand Montgomery to heel? Well, it seems that our fiendish duke has compromised me in the eyes of all London, and that Rand challenged him to a duel for it!"

"No! Then I wonder why I have not heard the rumors yet? I am always one of the first . . . are you certain, my dear?" Melinda asked with a frown.

"Yes, yes, of course I am! Rand told me that he and Worthington fought a duel because of it, and that the duke is laid up with a wound. Rand limps, and was not unhurt himself." She wrung her hands. "I am at a loss as to what to do, Melinda! If I admit that it was all a hoax to bring him to Kenilworth, he will know that . . . that . . . I care, and if I do not admit it, then he will think I have been compromised!"

"Quite a dilemma," her friend agreed. "What do you think we can do?"

"Short of murder, nothing," Jessamy said darkly. "I am undone."

"Nonsense! You must hold up your head, my dear! Do not let idle gossip affect you."

"That is easier said than done."

"Oh, of course." Melinda considered for a moment, then said, "I have it! You will attend my little party Saturday evening . . ."

"Oh no, I couldn't! Not now!"

"But of course you can. You will attend, and we will set buzzing tongues to rest, my dear. It is settled!" Melinda said cheerfully. "Now, where are those delicious little cakes you usually serve with tea?"

The weather cooperated beautifully with Melinda Fielding's party. It was cool enough for light wraps, and the sky was so clear that one could see the stars twinkling in benign complacence. Jessamy dressed carefully, paying strict attention to her choice of garments. She must look her best tonight, for she had devised a simple plan that should serve as the perfect catalyst to end the pretense between Rand and her concerning her relationship with Worthington.

A short note had been sent to Worthington, begging him to attend Lady Fielding's party even if he must be brought on a litter, and she had managed to coerce Rand into being her escort. A confrontation was the only way in which to scotch the rumors that must be flying as thick as bees in clover.

So Jessamy, garbed in a gown of the softest silk that was caught up just beneath her bosom with a wide ribbon of royal blue satin, descended the sweeping curve of stairs that led to the first floor, confident that her troubles would be over before midnight.

When they arrived at Field House, Rand was immediately ushered into Richard Fielding's study to view his collection of swords, while Jessamy was left in Melinda's capable hands.

"I received a message from Worthington," that lady said in hushed tones, pausing dramatically before adding, "he is to attend!"

"Perfect." Jessamy nodded in satisfaction. "Then we may rest easier, Melinda. Before the clock strikes twelve tonight, matters should be cleared."

"I hope so. Do you realize the risk you are taking?" Melinda asked anxiously. "I mean, having those two—who have already been at dagger-drawing—in the same house at the same time? What if there is another duel?" In spite of her fears, there was a definite note of suppressed excitement in Melinda's tone that made Jessamy smile.

"I hardly think they will go that route again, my dear. At the most, perhaps one of them will aim a leveler at the other, no more. I wish to avoid any such thing, of course. That is why I ask your assistance."

"But of course! What shall I do?"

Drawing Melinda to one side, well away from the open doors to the study, Jessamy quickly explained what was expected, enlisting her friend's aid in her plan.

"Plotting, ladies?" Richard Fielding boomed from the doorway, gaining their instant attention. "New jewels, I'll warrant," he added to Rand indulgently. "Melinda has a penchant for anything that glitters or sparkles. I vow, we would have an entire room filled with them if she had her way!"

Moving gracefully across the floor, Lady Fielding tucked her hand through her husband's elbow and gazed up at him affectionately.

"Pooh! You gave me almost all of my jewels, Chuffy, and you know it! I don't have an opportunity to buy anything!"

Rand and Jessamy exchanged amused glances at her affectionate term for her husband, but as more guests began arriving, they did not have an opportunity to speak for a time. It was only later, midway through the evening, that another chance for conversation occurred, and that was when the Duke of Lichfield chose to arrive.

"Worthington!" Rand muttered under his breath, stiffening. He cast an accusing glance at Jessamy. "Did you know he was to attend?"

"Yes, but I . . ."

Rand pivoted on his well-shod heel and stalked away, leaving Jessamy in mid-sentence. She chose to ignore the glances she was receiving from curious onlookers—and hoped that they would not gossip about that, too, though no one had made the least reference to her rumored indiscretion the entire evening—and followed Rand.

"We need to discuss this, Rand," she said, catching up to him and placing one small hand upon his coat sleeve. "Please—I knew you would not speak to him unless forced to, so I had to arrange a meeting like this."

Though about to refuse, Montgomery gazed down into Jessamy's beseeching face and surrendered. He found it exceedingly difficult to deny her anything, even knowing what he did about her tryst with Worthington.

"Very well. I am a sensible man. I can at least be civil," he said.

Jessamy's face brightened. "Excellent! Then let us step onto the terrace."

"I thought you wished to confront the duke . . . ?"

"Melinda is taking care of that detail for us, but I do not wish to converse with the duke in view of all of England, thank you! Shall we?"

They moved to the terrace, where Worthington had already been guided by Melinda Fielding. The duke, who possessed among his many other faults, the besetting sin of exquisite enjoyment of the ridiculous, waited upon them by a huge stone urn filled with geraniums.

"We meet again," he said pleasantly to Rand, bowing stiffly as he was still bandaged about the ribs. "Under better circumstances, I trust."

"Please," Jessamy begged, "I would like for you to explain matters to his lordship, Your Grace. Things seem to have gotten into a terrible coil, and I cannot see head from tail! Will you assist me?"

"But of course, fair lady." Worthington's eyes twinkled as he gazed at Jessamy. "You wish for me to tell him the truth—the *entire* truth?"

She nodded. "Oh, yes!"

"Then toddle off for a bit. I should like privacy while I talk to the earl, my dear. Give us five minutes."

Jessamy spent an agonizing half hour waiting for a summons, then gathered her courage and strode back to the terrace with great determination. Would Rand listen? Would he forgive her for her part in the hoax? And most of all, would he understand that it was only because she cared so much for him that she had even concocted such a scheme? It was a sobering thought to realize that she loved him.

Taking a deep breath, she stepped onto the stone-flagged terrace. It took a moment for her eyes to adjust to the dimmer light, and she paused, focusing at last upon the tall figure leaning on the stone balustrade beside the huge urn of geraniums.

"Lord Worthington?" she queried as she recognized the shadow. "Where . . . where is the earl?"

"No cause for alarm, dear Lady Jessamy. He has gone."

"Gone?" she echoed in bewilderment.

"Yes, gone back to Maryland."

"But . . . but . . ."

"Ah, there is no need for concern," Worthington assured her, lifting one arm and grimacing at the sudden spasm of pain that wracked him. "He has not taken your child with him, but left her in your care. I did convince him that she was best left with you instead of taken to America."

"He went home . . . alone?" Jessamy repeated, still unable to believe it. What had gone wrong with her careful plans? This was not at all what should have happened.

"Yes, he has gone."

Angrily now, Jessamy faced Worthington, her eyes blazing with sapphire sparks that would have cowed a more conscionable man. "Whatever did you say to him? I demand to know!"

"Why, did you not wish for your reputation to be restored, my dear? I had the impression that this was your immediate concern, as it was the earl's—"

"What," Jessamy repeated in a low tone, advancing upon the duke, "did you say to him?"

"Nothing, my dear, nothing but that I would marry you and thus restore your unblemished reputation."

✳ Chapter 19 ✳

It was a determined Jessamy who forced Lord Worthington back into his carriage to transport her to Kenilworth. She had no intention of allowing Rand Montgomery to leave without her. The short trip along the narrow roads between Field House and Kenilworth was fraught with accusations and explanation, and the duke sought to soothe Jessamy.

"I told you, my dear," he said wearily at one point, "it will do the earl a world of good to think that he has lost you to another man! Might wake him up. And really, don't you think that he should stew in his own juices? No? How unfortunate." He yawned, and peered through his quizzing glass at Jessamy. "I say, you are turned out most beautifully this evening, m'dear. Too bad you won't take me serious about my marriage proposal. I shall have to wed, you know, and you have been the most likely prospect."

"Don't try to wriggle out of our wager," Jessamy reminded sharply. "Wed some woman whom you've already compromised, and by the way—are you *certain* that Rand is the only one you told?"

Shrugging, Worthington sighed pensively. "Yes, the reluctant earl was the only one whom I told I had compromised you. And I received a devilish wound for it, too, may I add. Not a breath of scandal shall attach itself to you. I hope you appreciate my efforts."

"Of course I do—I think," Jessamy said, alighting from the elegant landau as soon as it paused in front of Kenilworth. She did not even wait for a footman to open the door, but sped up the steps with a brief wave of farewell to the duke.

"Dueced difficult," the duke murmured to no one, "that she cannot fall in love with me as she has that rustic. Oh well, no accounting for female taste, I suppose. Drive on," he called to his driver, and the landau jerked forward.

Disappointment dogged Jessamy, however, as she discovered that Rand had already left Kenilworth. Never one to accept defeat gracefully, she ordered a carriage brought around and prepared to follow him.

The curricle set off at a smart pace, bowling along the curving roads in pursuit of a single horseman. Dark shapes flitted past as Jessamy strained to see through the night shadows, holding her breath as the coachman took curves as fast as he dared, the curricle leaning dangerously. Her hands gripped the sides, knuckles white in the dark as she prayed they would overtake Rand.

A particularly difficult curve was taken on one wheel as the curricle balanced precariously, almost throwing Jessamy to the road, and she screamed. It was then that the wheel wobbled, and spun away from the vehicle into the night, leaving the curricle to be half dragged by the frightened horse. The coachman fought the plunging animal and bulky vehicle safely to the side of the road, and casting the reins aside, leaped back to see to Jessamy.

"My lady!" he gasped, face white in the dim light of a silver moon, "Are you all right?"

"Yes . . . yes, Painswick. I am unharmed." Sitting up and straightening her gown, which had been torn in the wreck, she gazed down the road, knowing that Rand could not be overtaken now.

Within two days Kenilworth was closed, trunks and portmanteaus packed, and passage secured on the next ship leaving for America. Margaret, who predicted doom, went about her tasks quietly for the most part, glancing now and then at Jessamy. The earl had been able to leave London immediately upon his return, and she had once more been foiled in her attempts to detain him. And this Jessamy was an entirely different Jessamy from the composed young lady who had sailed for America the previous spring. This time she hoped to capture more than the title to an estate. This time she intended to capture the heart of a man she had discovered that she loved above everything.

Not even the rough crossing disturbed Jessamy, and when they stood once more on the shores of Maryland, she somehow felt as if she were not a stranger any longer.

"Mummy!" Chastity cried, "shall we see Uncle Rand soon?"

"Yes, my pet," Jessamy answered, "very soon."

But Rand was not residing in his Baltimore house; he had returned to Idlewood. Jessamy waited, gathering her courage and resting, hoping that Rand would come to her when he discovered that she was in residence in his townhouse.

It was Corinne Blackwell who rescued her from sheer insanity as she waited, and Jessamy was grateful to the vivacious woman, who reminded her so much of Melinda Fielding.

"I think you should beard the lion in his den," Corinne commented, sipping at her tea. "He's only in hiding, you know."

"But you think that he would at least be curious as to why I have followed him," Jessamy said, staring gloomily across the small parlor. "Instead, he sends a short note telling the servants to see to my every need. Nothing for me, not even a casual query regarding my need of *him*!"

"What did you expect?" Corinne asked curiously. "Rand Montgomery has a great deal of pride, you know. Most men do, and he is no exception. From what you have told me, this duke did his feelings a great injury."

"But couldn't he have asked *me*?"

"Of course. But that would be too simple. And do men ever do anything simply?" Corinne took another sip of tea. "He's been invited to my affair tonight, of course, but I am certain he will not attend."

"Why?" Jessamy leaned forward eagerly. "Have you spoken to him?"

"No, but one of my overseers arrived in Baltimore today and mentioned that Rand was in the midst of a project at Idlewood that commanded a great deal of his time and attention. I hardly think he will come."

"What—or who—is the project, I wonder," Jessamy said bitterly, thinking of Selma Copley. Corinne, who had the uncanny ability to sense what Jessamy was thinking, looked up at her.

"Perhaps Miss Copley is hoping for the same thing you are, my dear."

"Yes. Perhaps she is," Jessamy murmured, sitting back in her chair. "Oh, I do so hope Rand will attend tonight!"

But Jessamy was doomed to disappointment. Rand did not attend Corinne Blackwell's dinner party, but sent a last-minute note declining, which cast a pall over the evening for Jessamy.

She left the party early, pleading a crushing headache that didn't fool Corinne for an instant. Alighting from the brougham in front of Rand's townhouse, Jessamy marched up the path without noticing all the front lamps had been lit, she was so lost in her own misery.

To her surprise, Wills opened the front door for her, his ebony face creasing into a wide, white smile.

"Welcome, ma'am," he said. "You been missed."

"Thank you, Wills! What . . . what are you doing here?"

"Mistah Rand done told me to come. Can I get you anything to eat, maybe, ma'am?"

"Oh no, thank you. I'm not at all hungry," Jessamy began, but another voice cut across hers, spinning her around.

"That's unusual," a deep, familiar voice drawled, and Rand appeared in the doorway to the small parlor, leaning a broad shoulder against the frame.

"Rand!" Jessamy's heart began to thud at an alarming rate.

"Ah, you've remembered me," he commented, flicking her with a warm, dark gaze that left her flustered.

"I . . . I . . . didn't expect to see you here."

"No?" A dark brow lifted. "This is my home, my lady."

"Yes, but . . . but I have been here a fortnight and have had no word from you."

"Idlewood has kept me busy after so long an absence, I'm afraid. And there were my merchant ships to see to, as well as a hundred other little details that have been lacking my supervision."

"And to what do we owe this pleasure now?" she asked, moving across the fine carpet on the parlor floor while Wills shut the door discreetly. Jessamy did not witness the broad wink and grin he gave Rand before leaving.

"I missed Chastity," Rand said. "Brandy?" He lifted a snifter and decanter and paused to slant her a questioning glance.

"Yes . . . yes, I will have some, thank you." Jessamy put her hands behind her so he would not see their trembling. "Have you seen Chastity yet?"

"No, she was asleep when I arrived. I will wait until the morning, since I intend to take her with me to Idlewood anyway."

"Pardon? I don't recall your asking my permission."

"You would deny her the visit?" Rand asked, handing Jessamy the snifter of brandy.

"She doesn't have to know you were here—" Jessamy began, but Rand forestalled her.

"But she wrote and asked me to come and get her. She wants to see Jimmy—and me." His eyes met hers deliberately, and Jessamy trembled.

"Is that correct?" she asked coolly, curling her fingers around the slender glass stem of the snifter. "I had no idea she'd written."

"I got the impression you were rather opposed to her visiting me."

Biting her lower lip, Jessamy recalled an earlier conversation with Chastity only the week before, when the child had begged to visit Idlewood. It could so easily have been misconstrued to mean that she did not wish her to see Rand or Jimmy.

"Oh, don't worry," Rand was saying, "she did not go behind your back to write me. Margaret helped her."

Jessamy's gaze shot to Rand. "Margaret?"

"Yes."

Stunned by such duplicity, Jessamy sank into a chair when it seemed as if her rebellious legs would no longer hold her upright. How had this happened?

"Jessamy," Rand was saying gently, and she looked up. "I have done what you wanted. Kenilworth is Chastity's."

Her voice came out a tiny squeak. "You . . . you . . . have given it to her?"

"Yes, my dear lady. I don't want an estate and title that means nothing to me. I have all I want here in Maryland, where I was born. England is beautiful, and I met some very nice people there, but America is my home."

"I don't understand . . . "

"I never wanted Kenilworth, Jessamy. I had planned to give it to Chastity even before I received your first letter."

"Then why . . . why did you allow me to . . . to come to America and . . . and . . . "

"And scheme so energetically?" he supplied helpfully. "I was enjoying the play entirely too much. Only virtuous men can deny themselves the pleasure of being amused by human foibles. Alas, I do not subscribe to such habits."

"You fiend," Jessamy said without rancor.

"Yes. And scoundrel, and 'cocklebrained,' I believe was one of the epithets you chose."

Jessamy colored hotly. "Your memory is too sharp, sir," she murmured.

"On some subjects, yes," the earl admitted. "But do not despair. I also remembered to see that you received your inheritance. You are quite wealthy."

"I do not need your money," she said stiffly.

"It is not my money. It is yours."

"I refuse to have you as benefactor—"

"Don't be a complete widgeon! The money belonged to your husband, not me. It was left you by the earl. Now don't be foolish and refuse it," he said when she began to sputter angrily. "You will need it for your dressmaker bills and your food—which, if I recall, should rival the debts run up by the Prince Regent."

Snapping to her feet, Jessamy slammed her snifter of brandy to a table and faced Rand with both hands on her hips, glaring at him.

"You despicable beast! How dare you mock me!"

"I am not mocking you, Jessamy. I am simply pointing out some of the more pressing reasons why you should accept my offer—"

"Do you think to buy me off and cast me from your life that easily, my lord?"

"Well, it certainly seems as if you cannot even manage to be wed!" he snapped. "I had thought you and Worthington a love match, yet now you show up on my doorstep like an abandoned puppy! Did you tire of one another so quickly, *duchess*?"

Furious at his taunting suggestion that she could not find a husband, Jessamy flung carelessly, "If you are so grieved that I have not wed, my lord, perhaps I should reinstate my earlier offer! I am certain you are still willing to settle a generous dowry upon me to attract suitors to such a drab creature as I am." Her blue eyes sparkled angrily, piercing him with accusation.

"Ah, so we are to test suitors with chess again, are we?" Rand asked, caught between amusement and fury. "How droll. I was right about one thing, Lady Jessamy Montgomery— you are not at all tedious like so many women. In fact, I shall enjoy watching you perform love's gambit."

✳ Chapter 20 ✳

The following weeks passed in a blur as Jessamy threw herself into an endless round of parties and various social engagements, most of which culminated with a lively game of chess. As usual, her opponents were disappointed and Baltimore highly entertained.

Margaret had taken Chastity to the country, leaving Jessamy in solitary residence. The old nurse had been beside herself when informed that Jessamy had once more begun her vulgar entertainment, and had so chastised her that it was a relief for both when the carriage departed for Idlewood.

Rand kept in touch through Wills, and the servant could only shrug when asked as to his master's location.

"I don' rightly know, ma'am. He moves about from Idlewood to his offices so much, an'... an' I just don' know."

Accepting this excuse calmly, Jessamy only nodded and said, "If he returns to his house tonight, you may tell him that I will be at Serena Chastain's dinner party. He may find me there if he wishes."

The Chastain dinner party was sumptuous, as usual, with a vast array of English dishes added in honor of their British guest. Roasted fowl rested beneath a blanket of béchamel sauce and tarragon, and soup á la Reine was followed by fillets of turbot with an Italian sauce; chicken á la Tarragon was flanked by a dish of spinach and croutons, glazed Virginia ham, chilled partridges with broiled mushrooms, and a raised mutton pie. Decidedly English, Jessamy declared, and quite delicious.

To satisfy less intrepid souls, the Chastains had served the more familiar roast beef, hot rolls, fresh broccoli and asparagus, carrots, peas, and a variety of fruit cobblers to tempt the palate. It was a splendid meal, and Jessamy partook of each dish with relish.

"I don't know how you stay thin as a stick and still eat so much," Corinne Blackwell complained good-naturedly. "I should rival the size of one of the colonel's ships if I attempted to consume that much food."

"Thin is not exactly the fad," Jessamy returned dryly. "Most men prefer women who have fuller figures."

"Not that gallant who just pleaded with me to see if you would consider playing him a game of chess. He has heard of your offer, of course—who has not?—and is intrigued."

"You don't approve," Jessamy said.

Corinne shook her head. "It does not matter to me. All that matters is the fact that you are desperately unhappy. Can you not mend the rift with Rand?"

Jessamy looked away, wishing it was that simple. "Each time we speak, we fight. I cannot seem to say the right thing, and he does not . . . does not care."

"Bother! The man adores you."

Jessamy's eyes widened incredulously. "Why do you say that?"

"Because it's true. You should stop trying to antagonize him with these chess games you persist in playing—uh-oh. Here comes Adonis," she said, referring to the young man who had been staring at Jessamy. "I see that he intends to beg a chess game from you himself. Jessamy, he is at least seven years younger than you . . . "

"But he is quite handsome, don't you think?" Jessamy teased, wondering if it was true that Rand loved her. Oh, if only he would declare himself!

"My lady," the golden young man was saying then, bowing before her like a French courtier, "may I be so bold as to present myself to you? I am Terrance Winthrop, from Charleston."

"Mr. Winthrop . . . " Jessamy allowed him to kiss her hand, then gently removed it from his grasp.

Standing, Winthrop nodded politely to Corinne, but his eyes remained on Jessamy. "Mrs. Blackwell," he murmured, then to Jessamy he said, "Are you still interested in playing chess games, my lady?"

"I take it that you are interested, Mr. Winthrop, but perhaps you don't understand the stakes," Jessamy began.

"No," he contradicted her, "I understand the stakes quite well."

"You are so young, Mr. Winthrop," she said delicately, "that I hesitate to accept your challenge."

"I look younger than my actual years, my lady. I have reached my majority."

Corinne put in, "Terrance Winthrop from Charleston? Aren't you staying in Selma Copley's house?"

He nodded. "She is still in the country, however. Her estate keeps her busy."

"I see," Corinne murmured with a meaningful glance at Jessamy.

Her point was well taken. Selma, in the country with Rand. How cozy, Jessamy thought with a sigh.

"My lady, I believe there is a chess board in the back sitting room," Terrance Winthrop was saying. "Care to try your fortune?"

"Jessamy," Corinne began, but Winthrop cut in.

"Do not worry. I think the lady intends to win all her games, and thus have no need of a husband."

Corinne's mouth drooped open, but Jessamy laughed. "You are much older than your years," she said to the young man, "and very shrewd. Do you think you can defeat me?"

"I should like to have a chance to prove my worth," he replied earnestly.

"With marriage as the prize? You seem too intelligent for idle games, and not at all hungry for a bride. Why would you wish to play?" she asked curiously.

Shrugging, he said, "We can play for other stakes, my lady. I simply wished to try to accomplish what many others have not been able to do."

"So what are the stakes?"

Pausing thoughtfully, Winthrop suggested, "Your diamond necklace, perhaps, and even a kiss?"

That suggestion brought Worthington and the disaster precipitated by Jessamy's careless wager back to mind, and she flinched. "What would you have to wager, sir?" she asked then, "since this is not a usual game?"

"My best horse," he said promptly, and Jessamy agreed. It was only a few minutes before they were seated at the chess board, which any Baltimore hostess in the know would provide since Jessamy's astounding proposal.

Jessamy had her back to the door and did not see Rand enter, but she recognized his voice when he stepped close to the table.

"Another game, my lady?" he said lightly, and Winthrop glanced up with a frown from arranging the playing pieces.

"Yes," she said shortly.

"And the wager . . . ?"

"My diamond necklace and a kiss against his best horse," she answered calmly, though her heart was thudding madly.

"How convenient."

Something in Rand's tone must have conveyed a sense of disquiet to Winthrop, for the young man rose from his chair and immediately offered it to the older man. "I insist," he said politely, sparing a regretful glance toward Jessamy.

Trapped, Jessamy had no choice but to play Rand, though she distinctly recalled the last time. She strained to recall his favorite opening—Caro-cann or Falkbeer counter gambit? Oh dear, it could have been the French defense, while her favorite was the Queen's gambit.

"What are the stakes, my lord?" she asked him politely, and he smiled.

"The necklace and kiss will do nicely, my lady."

The game began, the minutes ticking slowly past as they played to a growing crowd. Her knight forked, attacking his rook and a bishop, and Rand lost the bishop. The ormolu clock on the mantel ticked louder, and someone coughed, the noise raking across Jessamy's strained nerves. She glanced up irritably, and when she looked back at the board she saw that she had been double-checked. She must move her king or be checkmated. Stunned, Jessamy searched frantically for an alternative move, but she was trapped as neatly as a fish in a net.

"Your move," Rand purred, and she glared at him.

"I have none."

"Then . . . " He reached out, moving his piece, and said, "Checkmate."

✳ Chapter 21 ✳

Morning dawned bright and breezy, blowing in through the parted curtains to whisper across Jessamy's face in a gentle caress. Turning, Jessamy woke slowly, and realized that she had slept the entire night in her gown. She was aghast. Never had she done such a thing before! But never had she been so discouraged.

Rand was to collect his prize this morning, she remembered, sitting up and searching wildly for a clock. He must not find her like this!

Sara soon had Jessamy presentable, changing her frock and dressing her hair, though it took the best part of an hour of cold compresses to reduce the swelling of her eyes caused by crying. Sara had just put the last ivory pin in Jessamy's pale hair when Drucilla announced that the earl awaited Jessamy in the downstairs parlor.

"Tell him I will be there in a moment," Jessamy said. Her nerves were fluttering, and the mirror revealed a pinched look around her mouth and eyes. She had to calm herself, so she requested a small glass of port though it was only nine of the clock. Nine in the morning, yet she was drinking to gather her courage! Margaret would die of shame!

Finally ready, Jessamy smoothed her silk skirts, picked up the small velvet box containing her diamond necklace, and went into the hall.

Rand was waiting patiently in the parlor, and rose when Jessamy entered the room, giving a polite little bow. "I trust you spent a good night," he murmured.

But Jessamy was in no mood for idle pleasantries. "No, not really," she said. "If you must know, I spent a miserable night!"

Rand's brow rose inquiringly as he swept her with a wary glance. "A pity," he murmured in the same nonchalant tone.

"It certainly was!" was the instant rejoinder. Jessamy held out the velvet box. "Here is your prize, my lord."

A small smile hovered at the edges of Rand's mouth as he reached out for the box. Strong fingers grasped not only the velvet box but Jessamy's fingers, holding them firmly in his grip. "The diamonds are extremely nice, of course, but . . . "

"But what!" Jessamy snapped suspiciously. "Do they not suit you, my lord? Were you expecting the crown jewels, perhaps?"

"Diamonds are diamonds—just cold gems with no emotion, no feeling," Rand replied coolly. "I desire something warmer, with more emotion."

Jessamy gave a slight, futile tug at her captured hand, glancing up at Rand's face. "I don't know what you mean."

"I have made arrangements for you to join Chastity in the country."

"You wish for me to go to Idlewood?" Jessamy stared at him for a long moment, unable to believe the fact that Rand seemed actually to want her at Idlewood. After all, there was that little tangle with Worthington, wasn't there? Yet Rand still appeared to be in the dark about the details—how could she explain to him when it should have been the duke who explained? And would he even believe her? Or worse, be furious because of the deception?

"Do you not wish to go?" Rand asked with a trace of impatience in his tone.

"I don't know," Jessamy began hesitantly. Her conscience was still smarting, and she considered that it would be best to tell Rand the truth and suffer the consequences now instead of later.

"I see that you still harbor ill feelings," Rand commented wryly. "Or would you rather stay in Baltimore with your endless rounds of parties and teas . . ."

"I never claimed such a thing!" Jessamy said before she could halt her tripping tongue.

"Then you will come?"

"No."

"I see." Rand's mouth was thinned to a straight line, and his dark eyes were smoky with angry shadows as he turned to leave, but Jessamy yielded to impulse and reached out to touch his arm.

"Rand," she pleaded softly, "I . . . I need to tell you the truth."

Puzzled, he turned back to gaze at her. "I thought we had settled the matter of Kenilworth."

"Kenilworth is not what troubles me, though I have thought about it lately; there is another little matter."

Rand's eyes narrowed and he regarded her with a reluctant smile pressing at the corners of his mouth. "Why do I have the distinct impression that your 'little matters' always turn into grand gestures?" he murmured thoughtfully.

A timid smile curved her lips as Jessamy said, "You shouldn't tease. This is a serious matter."

"I can well imagine how serious it must be for you to want to admit 'the truth' to me," he muttered. "Since I have made your acquaintance there has been little but trouble between us."

Jessamy bridled immediately. "I consider that an insult! Don't you think that you are exaggerating the situation a great deal, sir?"

"And on which occasion do you think I've done that?" Rand inquired incredulously. "If anything, I have been the one who has attempted to keep some sort of logic and consistency in our dealings..."

"Logic? Consistency?" Jessamy echoed. "What logic can there be with a man like you? Can you answer that, pray tell?"

"Ahhh—this, my lady, is logical," Rand answered, reaching out in exasperation to draw her close. Bending his head, he pressed his mouth over her lips, lingering softly, aware of the slight expulsion of her breath as he kissed her.

Startled, Jessamy felt her head swim for a moment as she seemed to lose all reflexes. Instead, her breath mingled with his, and she wound her arms around his neck in response to his embrace, losing herself in the touch of Rand so close to her.

And when he pulled away moments later, instead of crying out with disappointment as she wanted, she said tartly, "I would hardly deem that logical or consistent, sir,"

Grinning, Rand shook his head. "I should have done that a long time ago—as soon as you began talking, in fact. It would have saved a great deal of time and talk."

"Blackguard!"

"Blackguard?" Rand's brows rose. "Doing it a bit strong,

aren't you? Bounder, perhaps, or even a rapscallion, but *blackguard*?'' He shook his head. ''Much too strong, my dear.''

Jessamy lost herself so far as to stamp one daintily shod foot on the thick carpet. ''I knew it would be senseless to attempt a discussion with you. That is the reason you and I always end up in a pickle—we cannot converse!''

''Kissing is infinitely preferable to conversation,'' Rand observed, his arms lifting as if to embrace her again.

But Jessamy moved swiftly out of arm's reach. ''Not so quickly, my lord.''

'' 'My lord' again? I thought we had that settled . . .''

''It might have been if you would be civil long enough for me to say what I must say.''

Crossing his arms, Rand leaned against a walnut table filled with an infinite variety of bric-a-brac and said, ''Suit yourself, Lady Jessamy. I hang upon your every word.''

Wringing her hands in an uncharacteristic gesture, she strained to form just the right words, finally settling upon, ''I must tell you something about the Duke of Lichfield.''

''Oh?'' Rand's tolerant smile disappeared at once. ''I do not believe we need to discuss your past . . . errors.''

''But that's just it,'' she said quickly. ''It is the fact that you consider it my error that we must discuss . . .''

Rand straightened, his face a stony mask as he gave her an icy gaze. ''You are wrong, madam. We have nothing to discuss.''

''But we do. You fought the duke, am I correct?''

''Fought him? Damme, woman, I almost killed him!'' Rand half snarled.

''If he had died, he would have died for nothing, sir,'' she said desperately.

''Nothing? It was obvious he thought so, but how can *you*

consider your tryst with Worthington nothing?'' Inhaling slowly the earl asked sarcastically, ''If it is not too much trouble, I would appreciate your explanation.''

''That's what I've been trying to give you,'' Jessamy began irritably, but at the look on Rand's face she added hurriedly, ''There was never anything between myself and the Duke of Lichfield, my lord, nothing but simple friendship.''

''Pardon?''

Clearing her throat, Jessamy repeated, ''We were nothing but friends—always.''

''I fought a duel with the man—''

''Of course you did! Worthington was certain you would do so—''

''Make yourself clear, madam, as I am rapidly losing patience,'' Montgomery warned in a tone that brooked no delay.

''Worthington came to me and proposed. I refused, and—''

''Oh. And he made up the rest of the story out of spite? Quite a Banbury tale, my dear, but I am not a man who is easily foxed with such.''

''No, no! Please listen,'' she begged. ''That was not it at all. I mean, it was, but let *me* finish the story without your assistance, please. Worthington proposed, I refused, and when he saw how distressed I was over the entire matter, he took it upon himself to concoct a plan. The duel was not what it appeared to be.''

''Pardon? I was there. I know what happened.''

''Oh, but you don't. Do you recall the kiss?'' she asked, and saw by his face that he did. ''Well, it was simply a kiss lost in a wager with him, that is all. He never compromised me at all. There was nothing between us, ever.''

''Then why did Worthington say all those ridiculous

things to incite me?'' Rand exploded, dark eyes narrowing. ''I find that amazing.''

''The duke created the entire drama so that you would come to the rescue of my good name...'' she began, unable to look at Rand anymore. She stared down at her twisting fingers forlornly. He would hate her now. He was furious and had a right to be, and why had she ever decided to confess to such a thing? She'd heard somewhere that confession was good only for those who confessed, never those who had to hear it, and now she believed it was true.

But to Jessamy's astonishment, she heard the faint, unmistakable sounds of laughter, low at first, then swelling to ripples of amusement that threatened to shake the chandelier. Her head came up and her eyes widened as she stared at Rand incredulously.

''What is so funny?'' she asked suspiciously.

''I was just considering the fact that I should have followed my first instincts and strangled him at the opera house that night. Then this entire matter would have been aborted before it began.''

''You aren't angry?''

''Oh, yes. I'm furious, but the entire situation is just so ludicrous that I find it difficult to take it seriously. How bored Worthington must have been to have whiled away his hours with this adventurous scheme,'' Rand marveled. ''He should really pay more attention to his estates and less to idle pleasure. It would give him a great deal more pleasure, and an immeasurable amount of wealth if he put as much effort into work as he seems to do Banbury tales.''

Jessamy peered at Rand narrowly. He seemed to be taking the matter extremely well—in fact, he was taking it a bit too well to suit her.

''It seems to me,'' she said loftily, ''that you would at

least be a tiny bit upset that Worthington could have ruined my reputation.''

''How could he manage that when you were a participant in his mad scheme, my dear?''

''Participant? Hardly! *Involved*, perhaps, but not an actual participant! I never knew the man intended to take his scheme as far as he did, and I was quite surprised and dismayed when I learned what he'd done.''

''Come, come,'' Rand protested with a smile, ''you must have known that he intended a duel—''

''No, I knew nothing! Even you should realize that I would never countenance so grave an act!''

''Hmm. Perhaps,'' Rand mused. ''But why did you and the duke go to all that trouble? What did you hope to achieve?''

''I told you, Worthington hoped that you would come to my rescue . . . ''

''So that he could politely kill me?'' Rand put in.

''No, and would you stop saying such things!'' Jessamy clenched her fists and glared at him. ''It was nothing of the sort! I wanted you to *care* for me,'' she blurted before she could stop herself, then added in a resigned whisper, ''The duke realized that I could never love him when I was fond of another man, so he was obliging enough to help me. That is all.''

Rand's gaze grew pensive. ''I see.'' Pivoting, he strode toward the long window and stood staring into the streets of Baltimore, watching carriages and passersby without really seeing them.

Disturbed by his silence, Jessamy grasped the edge of the walnut table until her knuckles grew white with tension. The small, forgotten velvet box lay carelessly on the table, a reminder of the reason for Rand's visit to her.

"I tried to explain to you," she began softly, "and I asked the duke to attempt an explanation, but instead . . . That is the reason I called him to the house that day. I wanted to end the deception." When Rand continued his stiff silence Jessamy crossed the short distance that separated them and reached out to touch him gently on the shoulder. "I apologize, Rand. I did not mean to deceive you."

"But you did, nonetheless," he pointed out quietly.

Jessamy's hand dropped away. "I never meant to hurt you."

"Ah, but perhaps there is a small moral to this tale, my lady," he said with forced lightness. "Playing games can be dangerous, if not deadly."

"And you have never played them, my lord?"

He shook his head. "Not like this."

"But you consented to my wager with marriage as the prize, and you also sponsored me with a dowry for the lucky suitor," she defended herself.

"I only wanted you to be happy—and married," he said.

"Yes—*married*." Jessamy gazed at Rand with determined eyes. "This tangle grew out of your determination for me to have a husband—any husband—when all I wanted was you," she said boldly, scarcely able to believe that she had dared so much.

He gazed at her for several long moments, and Jessamy could not read the expression in his eyes. Her heart fluttered like the wings of a trapped bird when he took a step toward her, then stopped to say, "You took your time saying this, my dear Jessamy." His hand lifted, then dropped to his side again. "I'm leaving for Idlewood this afternoon. If it pleases you, be packed."

Jessamy stood like a stone statue as he smiled at her,

turned, and walked away, pausing by the walnut table to remove the velvet box on his way out of the door.

"Rand . . . " she said, but it was too late. He was gone. If he heard her call, he said nothing. She stood there until she heard the faint, unmistakable sounds of his horse's hooves on the cobblestones of the street fade way. Shaking her blond head, Jessamy despaired, "A fine mess this has all turned out to be! I shall never play chess again . . . "

✳ Chapter 22 ✳

Gowns, reticules, shoes, shawls, and bonnets were packed, and the many hatboxes Jessamy had collected were stacked vertically inside the coach. She descended the sweep of stairs slowly, holding up the hem of her skirts with one hand so that she would not trip, her mind on the journey's end.

She would grasp this opportunity to speak frankly with Rand, Jessamy decided. After all, they were traveling together, and there would be ample time. Perhaps by the end of the ride they would have matters straightened out between them.

Pausing in front of the huge gilt mirror in the downstairs hallway to glance at her reflection, Jessamy drew a deep breath to steady her nerves. No strain showed on her face, and she was satisfied that no one would guess the depth of her worry over her relationship with Rand.

"Good morning, Boris!" she said gaily to the coachman waiting upon her arrival outside the front door. The smile remained on her lips as she pulled on her cotton gloves, even when she noticed that Rand was not yet present.

"Where is your employer?" she asked nonchalantly, as if the answer did not matter in the least. Surely he would go with her!

"Mister Rand will be back 'round shortly, ma'am. He got a bit impatient with waiting, and rode back to the stables to check a loose curb chain on his bridle."

Jessamy frowned. Then that meant that Rand was riding his stallion instead of inside the carriage. Then how could she talk with him? Biting her lower lip, she briefly contemplated several options before Rand appeared, riding around the curve in the drive and up to the house.

"Wouldn't you like to ride with me?" she asked. "We could tie your stallion to the back..."

"No. I prefer riding," he said bluntly. "Have you packed everything? Good God, I should think so," he added unnecessarily, eyeing the multitude of hatboxes.

"Yes," she muttered through clenched teeth, accepting the offer of Boris's hand to ascend the carriage step. She settled herself into the velvet cushions with a last irritated glance at Rand, and grabbed at her new chip-straw hat as the vehicle lurched to a start down the drive.

The well-sprung carriage rolled along the road meandering its way through rolling fields and grassy meadows, shaded by towering oaks, pines, and poplar trees, and serenaded by the cheerful chatter of bluejays, finches, and robins. The air was warm and sweet with the fragrance of honeysuckle and magnolia blossoms, and with the warm sun beaming down Jessamy grew drowsy.

Miles passed without incident or an opportunity to speak to Rand. When they paused to water the carriage horses and Jessamy got down from the carriage to stretch her legs, she approached Rand, but he scurried away as quickly and politely as possible. Frustrated, she watched him walk away, hands on her hips, vowing to corner him before the day was over.

Misfortune presented the perfect chance a scant hour later when the carriage suddenly lurched to one side, throwing Jessamy against the door. It happened so quickly that she didn't have time to scream at the violent motion, but found herself lying upon her side, pressed against the closed door as the carriage tilted to lie upon the ground.

Realizing a wheel or axle must have broken, she took quick stock of her bones and gave a thankful sigh of relief. Nothing was broken, she could feel no pain and didn't seem to be bleeding, but she *was* buried beneath several dozen hatboxes. Her hat had been knocked askew in the accident, and Jessamy could not see for the obstruction over one eye. When she tried to lift her arm, she found it confined by an overlarge cylinder containing her three best hats.

"Jessamy!" a voice called loudly, though she could barely hear for the fur and feathers piled atop her willy-nilly. "Jessamy!"

"Here," she called faintly, sputtering at a mouthful of feathers—ostrich feathers from her best hat!

"Jessamy, dear God, where are you!" the familiar voice called again, and she recognized Rand.

"Here!" she called more loudly, spitting at the clinging bits of feathers in her mouth. "Under the hats!"

"Oh dear God, will you look at this mess?" she heard Rand's disembodied voice say, and frowned at the amusement in his tone. This was not a bit funny. Hats were expensive, and besides, where could she get more hats like these in America?

A square of light appeared as a hatbox was removed from above her head, and Jessamy squinted up at Rand. "Are you well, my lady?'' he asked formally, and she bit back a tart answer.

"Quite well, thank you," she returned, "except for the fact that my velvet bonnet with the ostrich feathers seems to have taken flight. Would you mind?'' She wiggled her fingers helplessly.

"Not at all," he answered politely, reaching down through the small door window to free her. "Ah, what have we here?'' he murmured. "A blue silk, a lovely jonquil bonnet, a pink-and-white straw—''

"We can take inventory later," Jessamy snapped, wriggling uncomfortably.

"You're not injured, are you?"

"No, but I am stuck quite well."

"Stuck?'' he echoed. "Can you not move at all?''

"No. My dress seems to be caught on something, and even though you have removed the hatbox, all my weight is on one arm so that I cannot maneuver at all.''

"Do be still, then—''

"How do you suppose I could do anything else, you twit!'' she snapped again.

"Twit?'' Rand's brows rose. "My, my! Somehow I had cast myself in the role of white knight, rescuer, hero— certainly not *twit*.''

"Oh, Rand,'' Jessamy moaned, closing her eyes, but he was already removing the last obstruction and lifting her from her supine postition inside the wrecked carriage and into his arms. He balanced himself, holding Jessamy.

"Sorry, pet. I had to keep you talking so that you would not move and tilt the vehicle," he apologized. "I just wanted to divert you from what we were doing. Are you certain you are not injured?'' he added anxiously, his hands skimming over her arms in rapid examination.

She thought a moment. "No, I am not hurt. Just get me out of here—and don't trample my hats!" she added when his foot snared a bonnet.

"Damn your hats," the earl mutterded fiercely. He was holding her in his arms, standing inside the overturned vehicle with his head sticking out the opened side door, and heedless of who might be watching, Rand Montgomery gave her a quick, hard kiss. Jessamy gasped, not having expected such a reaction, but Rand was already gathering her up and handing her to Boris, who stood outside with a carefully blank expression on his face.

"You're light as a feather, ma'am," the coachman commented as he set Jessamy carefully upon the roadside.

"Don't you mean *covered* with feathers?" Jessamy observed with a wry laugh, glancing down at her gown. It was dotted with fluff and feathers of all colors and sizes, clinging to her in spite of her efforts to brush them away.

"You look rather like a large sparrow," Rand offered, clambering out of the ruined carriage.

"Thank you, my lord. I choose to take that as a compliment, since I rather admire the noble little bird." Jessamy gazed sadly at the carriage. "What are we to do now?"

"No matter," Rand said cheerfully. "We're only eight miles from Idlewood—"

"Eight miles?" Jessamy stared at him in horror. "It is much too great a distance for me to walk. I shall wait here."

"My dear Lady Jessamy, as much as I would like to grant your request, I find it impossible. Boris must stay with the horses. They are too fine a team to lose to some wayward thief. If you stay, it may be tomorrow before help can return for you. Do you wish to spend the night upon the road?"

Jessamy shuddered. "No, of course not."

"Then it is all settled."

"What is all settled?" she demanded warily.

"We shall ride to Idlewood on my mount."

"On *that* horse?" Jessamy gazed at the magnificent sorrel in horror. It had been said that no one but Rand could ride the animal, that the stallion would allow none other on his back. Now Rand was calmly proposing that she ride him! "I cannot," Jessamy refused.

"But you have no alternative, madam." Rand's voice was sharp. "And the longer we stand here discussing our options, the longer poor Boris must wait without food or water for our return. Do be cooperative for once, and step this way." Rand motioned her toward the stallion with an impatient wave of one hand.

Reluctantly conceding defeat, Jessamy took several unwilling steps toward him. It was not that she didn't know how to ride, for she was an expert horsewoman, it was just that she had had experiences with animals who did not care for two people upon their backs. It could end in disaster, and she wasn't certain that even Rand could control such a large stallion. The sorrel was observing her with rolling eyes and flaring nostrils, and she paused.

"Come along," Rand coaxed impatiently, and she put one hand into his palm.

"I shall be killed," she remarked resignedly, and he had the bad manners to laugh.

"I am more skilled in riding than you may think, my dear," he said. "Shall I give you a leg up?"

"Please refer to them as *limbs*," she said primly, biting back the tart words she really wished to utter.

"Fine. Shall I give you a limb up?"

Flashing him a sour glance, Jessamy nodded, put one foot in the palm of his hand and the other upon his shoulder, and stepped onto the broad back of the horse. Her skirts bunched quite immodestly around her knees, but Rand was gracious enough to look the other way while she smoothed them back down. Jessamy perched precariously upon the saddle—which was not made for a lady to ride sideways—and took a deep breath.

"Take this, Boris," Rand was saying, handing the coachman a pistol from beneath his coat. "You may not need it, but one can never tell. We shall send someone back for you immediately."

"Yes, sir," Boris replied imperturbably. He had already removed the coach horses from their traces and had them on leads, grazing the lush green grass along the roadside. "I shall be here."

Rand stepped into his saddle, catching Jessamy as she struggled for balance, and nudged the nervous sorrel into a walk.

"He doesn't like me," Jessamy commented as the stallion tossed his head and snorted his displeasure.

"But I do." Rand's lips were only inches from her ear, and she could feel his warm breath stirring tendrils of hair upon her neck.

Jessamy swallowed, and managed to say lightly, "Then I suppose that should be enough."

She could feel Rand's arm tighten around her as he held the leather reins in one hand, his other arm circling her slender waist to hold her upon the horse. The afternoon sun had mellowed with time, and was smiling down more benignly now, hiding behind the tops of the trees. Katydids rasped in the tall grasses alongside the road, and bees hummed their summer song as they toiled endlessly. The slow clop of the sorrel's hooves on the thick dirt of the road was rhythmical, and Jessamy began to feel comfortable at last. A small smile hovered at the corners of her mouth.

"Rand," she murmured, resting her head against his shoulder, "perhaps this accident can help us start anew."

"What do you mean?" he drawled, his breath tickling her ear again.

"Oh, just . . . I know you were—and still are—angry about Worthington, but . . ."

"Worthington is of no consequence," Rand said quietly.

"Then it must be something else that leaves us as strangers."

Rand was silent, and Jessamy could feel his weight shift behind her. She swallowed a sigh, wondering what she could do, then gave a mental shrug. There was nothing. Only time and Rand Montgomery could help the situation now.

"Are we almost there?" she asked a few moments later.

"Another hour at this pace," Rand answered. His big hand brushed against her waist. "Are you in a hurry?"

"Oddly enough, no. This is quite pleasant, and your horse has not tried to bolt as I feared."

"Then let's enjoy the ride," Rand murmured. "The country is beautiful at this time of the year, and Idlewood especially so. I imagine that Chastity and Jimmy are brown and rosy from playing outdoors all day . . ."

"Yes, and I can almost smell Polly's cooking," Jessamy added with a smile.

Rand laughed. "Food! The subject is never far from your mind—unless you are thinking of hats."

Laughing at his jest, Jessamy agreed. "But it takes a great deal of food to satisfy me, and Polly seems to make a special effort to prepare the dishes I enjoy."

"She'll be pleased to see you again, Jessamy."

"And I will be pleased to see her," she said softly.

"Jessamy—"

"Rand—" They both spoke at the same time, paused, and laughed.

"You first," he said then.

"I was just going to say that you seem much more accessible to me today than you ever have before. It's almost as if you truly like me."

Rand's tone was surprised. "But I *do* like you. And I have always been accessible to you, Jessamy."

"Especially when you were trying to find me a willing husband," she teased.

He gave a rueful laugh. "Well, I'm afraid you will have to find your own husband now, Jessamy. I am finished with my efforts at matchmaking."

"And I am finished playing chess."

"Perhaps I can teach you a new game?" he suggested. "Backgammon, perhaps?"

"Wonderful! I've never learned how to play," she said promptly.

"Wayne Copley would enjoy playing with us. He would welcome an opponent other than myself," Rand said casually, and noted Jessamy's tension.

"I . . . I am afraid that Mr. Copley might prefer company other than mine," she murmured. "We didn't seem to get along, you know."

"Yes, I know," he said gently, "but you must understand why Wayne is so bitter. It's his own history and has nothing to do with you. I cannot abandon him, Jessamy. I only hope that his personal torment will ease one day."

"I understand, Rand, truly I do. But wouldn't the war always be between us?"

"The war is over. It has been over for some time. I harbor no resentment now, Jessamy. We have all suffered enough for it and must learn to have done with old pain.

Maryland is my home, and I never want to leave. My life is here.''

Jessamy understood what he did not say, the meaning behind his words. If she stayed, America would be her new home, and she would never return to England to live. It was a choice she would have to make.

✳ Chapter 23 ✳

Dark lay on the land in soft, lingering shrouds when Jessamy and Rand arrived at Idlewood. Polly, with her all-knowing eyes, spotted them when they trotted up the end of the long, curving drive. She stationed herself immediately on the edge of the brick porch, a lantern held high in one hand.

"Mistah Rand, I been fit to be tied!" she scolded as they drew within hearing range. "I been wringin' my hands, pacin' the floors, and worryin' about you two. I knew you were supposed to come back today, and now it's past dark, and . . . why, where's the carriage? What done gone and happened?"

Rand reined in his sorrel, grinning down at Polly. "The carriage lost a wheel and turned over, Polly. Now don't go into a fit," he added quickly as the older woman's face creased in horror. "No one was hurt—"

"Except for my hats," Jessamy sighed mournfully.

Rand cocked his brow and continued, "And I left Boris with the team. Please tell Wills to gather up some help and go back for him. Oh, and you'd better send some food and water for Boris. I imagine he's pretty hungry by now."

"I reckon he is!" Polly said, shaking her head. "And I know you two are bound to be parched and starvin'. Come on in here, and I'll see to all of you. Mmm-hmm! Don't know what you'd do without me to see to all of you, I surely don't." Pausing, she rested her hands upon her wide hips and fixed Jessamy with a stern look. "And it's about time you showed up back here, little lady! This is where you belong, and it's 'bout time that someone *else* realized that, too!" She winked broadly, her smile wide and white in the dim light. "So you done rode through the dark all alone tonight, have you? I'd bet that will set some tongues a'waggin' when they find out, don't you reckon? Now don't be lookin' at me like that, Mistah Rand. I knows when to keep my mouth shut, and when to talk. Right now, I'll be puttin' some food on the table for you two right away," she said over her shoulder.

Polly bustled off as Rand swung down from his horse and threw the reins to a waiting boy, then reached up for Jessamy. His hands circled her slender waist as he lifted her down easily, his mouth slightly grazing her ear as she swung forward.

"I think Polly's glad to see you," he whispered, and Jessamy smiled.

"I think you're right," she whispered back. "What did she mean about wagging tongues?"

"By tomorrow," Rand said, setting Jessamy firmly on her feet, "I will have compromised you. After all, we just rode twenty miles—eight of them alone—through the countryside without benefit of a chaperone or maidservant, and now you have arrived home after dark. All the servants will be whispering behind their hands before morning, and soon it will be known at Fairoaks, Willow Lane, Finis Terre—''

''Do you mean that I have been compromised again?'' Jessamy interrupted as they entered the house.

''I do.''

''Why, Rand Montgomery! If I didn't know better,'' she teased, ''I would think you planned for that wheel to fall off!''

''It was not the wheel. The axle broke, but I still didn't plan that either,'' Rand said. ''This time, fate stepped in and did me a good turn, even though I'm an American and not English.''

''Really? How do you come to that surprising conclusion?'' Jessamy asked as they walked down the long hall to the back veranda. Rand was silent as they crossed from the main house to the low brick building that housed the kitchen. They paused for a moment on the tiled path leading from the house, and Jessamy turned to look up at Rand. It was quiet in the small kitchen garden where Polly grew a variety of fresh herbs, and the air was thick with the faint fragrance of rosemary, thyme, and sage.

''Rand,'' she prompted as they stood there in the dark, ''why do you think fate did you a good turn?'' She could see his smile in the dim light.

''Because it gave me an opportunity to realize how much I enjoy holding you in my arms, and how empty they would be if I could not do so,'' he replied softly.

''Then as I see it,'' she said briskly, ''there is only one solution to the matter.''

''And that is?''

''You must marry me at once, so that my reputation is not in shreds and my heart is not broken.''

He pulled her to him, cradling her chin in his palm, his

expression so tender that her eyes widened to huge blue pools. "It would break your heart if I did not?"

"I vow that it would break my heart if you were to give me a set-down," Jessamy said candidly.

Rand folded her into his embrace, holding her so closely that she could smell the special fragrance he wore, and feel his heart beating beneath the cheek she had pressed against his chest.

"My silly goose," he murmured against her hair, "I could never let you go. Do you know how frenzied I was when you were carrying on your mad scheme of wedding a man who could beat you at chess? I cannot tell you the hours of agony that I endured."

Jessamy smiled against his coat. "Really? Then it worked."

"Oh yes, you termagant! It worked! But I had to know if you wanted me more than you wanted Kenilworth, my dear. And I had to know if you could find it in your heart to live here at Idlewood. This is my home."

"I would live in a teacup with you if that is what you wished," Jessamy said simply, and Rand tilted back her head to search her eyes.

"I believe you would," he said in quiet astonishment. "But what about Kenilworth?"

"You gave it to Chastity, remember? It will be hers to do with as she wishes one day, just as I always wanted. Oh, I love the estate, but it belongs to the Montgomerys. Now, all of us will benefit."

Rand chuckled. "I can think of three people right now who will benefit."

Jessamy, watching the way his eyes crinkled when he laughed, and the disarming way his mouth turned up higher on one side than the other, asked distractedly, "And who are they?"

"Margaret, Polly, and Chastity," was the prompt reply.
"Margaret?"

"Oh, yes. She instructed me most sternly to bring you to your senses—"

"The traitor," Jessamy observed fondly. "And did she coach you in your chess game, also?"

"No, she didn't have to do that. If I had beat you, my love, you would never have known if you loved me. This way, you have an option. You may say yes to becoming my wife, or say no—"

"Yes," she said promptly. "Yes, yes, yes!"

Rand swung her around, kissing her soundly, then set her rather breathlessly back on her feet. "I love you," he said. "Let's forget eating and drink a toast instead. I have some excellent champagne in the cellar—"

"Why don't we have some of Polly's crepes with our champagne?" Jessamy suggested innocently.

Laughing, Rand made the wry observation that he would always wonder if she had married him for himself or his cook, but Jessamy only smiled.